Legends of Micronesia

BOOK ONE

Text by EVE GREY
Illustrations by TAMBI LARSEN

Fredonia Books
Amsterdam, The Netherlands

Legends of Micronesia
(Book One)

by
Eve Grey

ISBN: 1-4101-0266-1

Reprinted from the 1951 edition

Fredonia Books
Amsterdam, The Netherlands
http://www.fredoniabooks.com

Acknowledgments

For information and materials, thanks are given to young men and women of Micronesia and their elders who gave help in collecting the legends. Temporary residents and travelers in the South Pacific islands also have given assistance. Among several versions of some legends, preference was given to forms known to young people of today. Details in illustrations for legends are always controversial. The artist had to work without picture records of the ancients, having for reference only drawings and photographs of much more recent times. Since there are different languages and customs in Micronesia, the legends have been checked for local detail and spelling by the following men and women, who also furnished legend material:

The Marshall Islands : Lieutenant Commander H. W. Buckingham, Chaplain, USN, Kwajalein; Lokrap of Ailinglaplap; Dwight Heine, Superintendent of Elementary Schools; Amata Kabua, Instructor, Intermediate School; *The Eastern Caroline Islands:* Napoleon De Fang, Superintendent of Elementary Schools, Truk District; Robert Halvorsen, Educational Administrator, Ponape District; *The Western Caroline Islands:* R. Uag, Superintendent of Elementary Schools, Yap District; Alfonso Rebohong, Superintendent of Elementary Schools, Palau District; David Ramariu, Principal, Koror Elementary School, Palau District; *The Mariana Islands:* Mrs. Agueda I. Johnston, Assistant Superintendent of Schools, Guam; William Reyes, Superintendent of Elementary Schools, Northern Mariana Islands.

Acknowledgment for legend material is also given to the following inhabitants of Micronesia. *Marshall Islands:* Jonathan Mote, of Ebon; *Eastern Caroline Islands:* Bailey Otter, of Mokil; Samson Albert and Stewo Pelep, of Ponape; Simeon Aaron and Benjamin Isaiah, of Kusaie; Ahpel Ionis, of Pingelap; Lydia Selifies, of Truk; David, the late king, Kiati, and Rimari, of Kapingamarangi, for stories given to Samuel H. Elbert; *Western Caroline Islands:* Pitmag Louis and David Dabuchiran, of Yap; Francisco Morei, Akiwo, Toribiong Uchel. Toribiong Gorong, Yakop Sawaichi, Tarkong Pedro, and F. Ichikawa, of Palau; *Mariana Islands:* Sebastian Muna, of Saipan; and others.

For their interest and support, which made the book possible, gratitude is extended to Admiral Arthur W. Radford, USN, Commander in Chief, U. S. Pacific Fleet and former High Commissioner of the Trust Territory of the Pacific Islands; to Rear Admiral Leon S. Fiske, USN, former Deputy High Commissioner of the Trust Territory of the Pacific Islands; and to Lieutenant Commander Irwin K. Vandam, USNR, former Director of Education for the Trust Territory of the Pacific Islands.

Appreciated also are assistance and encouragement given by members of the Advisory Committee on Education for Guam and the Trust Territory: Mr. Oren E. Long, Governor of Hawaii, Dr. K. C. Leebrick, former Vice-President, University of Hawaii, Dean Harold A. Wadsworth, University of Hawaii, Dr. Kenneth P. Emory, Bernice P. Bishop Museum, and others; also Dr. S. H. Elbert, University of Hawaii; Margaret Titcomb, Librarian, Bernice P. Bishop Museum; Mrs. Margaret Hoeber, translator; and others.

CONTENTS

Animal and Bird Stories

Stories about Girls and Boys

CONTENTS—Continued

Stories about Ghosts and Giants

Stories about Parents and Children

Animal and Bird Stories

The people of Micronesia told many legends about animals. Among them were stories about the mouse, the rat, the crab, and the lizard. There were only a few land animals in the islands. The people spent much time on the water and knew a great deal about sea animals. Stories were told about the crab, the eel, the clam, the turtle, the octopus, the whale, and different kinds of fish.

There were many birds in Micronesia. Some legends told about birds that looked odd, that had strange cries, or that lived in secret ways. The frigate bird, large and fierce-looking, was a favorite bird of legend. It flew very high, and it had feeding and nesting places far from the villages of the people.

A sea bird of many colors that traveled over the ocean and had a sad, lonely cry was often told about in stories. No one found its nest, for it came from far away. Some people said that it flew to the top of the sky and dropped its egg, which fell for many days. Before it got to earth, out came a bird, which flew away without touching the ground. Sometimes, the bird cried at night, like a lost soul, telling the people something that was about to happen.

Some of the animal stories which the people told were short and funny. Some of them were long and exciting. In many legends, there was a lesson about good and evil. There were legends about animal ancestors of the people and their wonderful deeds. Sometimes, a good storyteller made the stories exciting by acting the parts of the animals and the people.

Here are some Micronesian legends with animal or bird heroes.

The Crab and the Needlefish

Fish is a favorite food in the Pacific Islands. When it has been wrapped in green leaves and baked among hot stones, it is delicious. But the children of the Mortlock Islands, in the Truk District, sometimes will not eat needlefish, for it has a bitter taste.

"Never mind, it's good food," their parents say. Then they tell the children why the needlefish tastes bitter.

The needlefish is smooth and slender, and he can swim very fast. He has a long, sharp needle sticking out in front, ready to spear anything that gets in his way.

One day, the needlefish saw a tiny sand crab crawling along the beach. The needlefish made fun of the crab.

"How slow and clumsy you are!" he said. "Watch me. See how fast I move through the water." He swam and dived and turned about with great speed.

The little crab watched the needlefish for a while, and then he said, "You're fast, needlefish, and I'm very slow, that's true. But just the same, I feel sure that I can beat you, if we have a race along the shore."

"Foolish talk!" cried the needlefish. "How could you beat me in a race? I go like lightning, and you crawl so slowly."

The little crab said, "Let's have a race tomorrow morning. We'll start here, beside this rock. I'll race you to the big *maras* tree that stands at the edge of the water, far down on the beach. You can swim in the water, and I'll crawl along on land."

The needlefish laughed and laughed, but he agreed to race with the little crab. "You're so tiny," he said. "How shall I know where you are?"

"That will be very easy," replied the crab. "Just call to me, now and then, and I'll answer you."

The needlefish swam away, still laughing.

Now the sand crab was small, but he was clever. He crawled along the beach all night long, telling his crab friends about the race. "The needlefish boasts too much. I want to teach him a lesson," he said.

He asked his friends to sit at different places near the water. They would be a few yards apart from each other, all the way between the rock and the *maras* tree.

"Tomorrow, the needlefish will call to me," he said, "to find out where I am. Each time he calls, one of you must answer for me. The needlefish will think that it is I who am ahead of him all the way."

The crab's friends thought it was a wonderful idea. They agreed to do what he asked.

Next morning, the little crab and the needlefish met at the rock and began the race. The needlefish swam off like lightning, but the little sand crab sat still. "It's my turn to laugh," he said, and so he laughed.

Before long, the needlefish called out from the water, "Crab, crab, where are you?"

On the shore, a small voice answered, "Here I am, just ahead of you!"

The needlefish was so surprised that he nearly jumped out of the water. He swam faster than ever. After a while, he called out again, "Crab, crab, where are you?"

Again a crab voice replied, "Here I am, just ahead of you!"

That time, the needlefish nearly broke himself in two, trying to swim still faster in the water. He kept on calling out, "Crab, crab, where are you?" And always, there was a little voice saying, "Here I am, just ahead of you!"

The needlefish was nearly out of his mind with anger. He raced so fast that the water whirled around him. When he reached the *maras* tree, there sat a little sand crab with a shell on his back. He was not at all tired.

"Well, needlefish, are you here at last?" said the crab.

The needlefish nearly burst with anger. He sprang out of the water with such force that his long needle stuck in the *maras* tree. There he hung for a long time. At last, he got the needle out again and dropped back into the water.

He swam away, feeling foolish. He tried to forget about the race, but he couldn't, for some of the bitter juice of the *maras* tree was in his mouth. It stayed there, to teach him not to boast too much.

Ever since that day, the flesh of the needlefish has had a bitter taste. As the Trukese people say, *"Much me sop me teremeimei,"* or, *"That's the end of the story."*

The Lobster and the Flounder

People in the Pacific Islands told how certain fish got their odd shapes. Some of the stories are very old and have been told hundreds of times. This is the way one of them is told in the atoll of Kapingamarangi, in the Eastern Caroline Islands.

A lobster and a flounder lived in the same lagoon. At that time, the flounder was just a common-looking fish. One day, the lobster said to the flounder, "Let's play hide-and-seek. I know good places to hide in."

"Very well," said the flounder, "you hide. Call out when you are ready, and I'll look for you."

The lobster hid behind a rock and shouted, *"Kamiro!"* The flounder found him right away and laughed.

"Why do you laugh?" asked the lobster.

"I'm laughing at you," replied the flounder. "You hide yourself, but you forget that your long antennas are sticking out. I can see them easily."

"So that's why you're laughing," said the lobster. "Well, suppose you go and hide, now."

The flounder swam away, and he played a trick on the lobster. He went to the middle of the lagoon, stirring up mud as he went. It clouded the water, so that the lobster couldn't see what the flounder was doing. The flounder pretended to hide in the center of the lagoon, but he came back in a roundabout way to the place where the lobster was waiting. Then he called out softly, "*Kamiro!*"

The lobster had seen the flounder swim toward the center of the lagoon, so he went there. He hunted for him in the cloudy water.

"I can't find you!" he shouted. "Call out again."

The flounder called, "*Kamiro!*" That time, the lobster listened, and he found where the sound came from. He went back to the old place, and there was the flounder, laughing at him.

The lobster was angry. "I went where I thought you were," he said. "Why did you fool me?"

"So that you wouldn't find me," said the flounder.

"You don't play fair!" cried the lobster, angrily. Then he went to the flounder and trampled upon him until the poor fish was quite flat.

"Now I'm leaving you!" he shouted. "And I won't play that game again!"

"Come back here!" cried the flounder. "You've hurt me and changed me completely. Make me the same as I was before."

The lobster returned. "What are you yelling about?" he asked.

"Why, you've spoiled my shape!" said the flounder. "Do you think you're playing fair? I have to swim flat now, with one eye to the ground, and the dirt gets into it. You'll have to do something about it!"

"Very well," said the lobster, who was still angry.

He looked at the eyes of the flounder. He saw that one of them was now on the under side. "I'll put it on top, where it will be out of the mud," he said.

And so he did. He dug it out and put it on the same side as the other eye. "I won't give you back your shape," he said. 'I've made you flat, so that people will step on you."

"Why, you wicked thing!" exclaimed the flounder. "You've made me flat. And now you're leaving me that way, are you? Well, I'll swim close to the bottom and stir up dirt, and people won't see me. As for you, ha, ha! You still have those long antennas. People will always see you and catch you!"

And so it has been ever since. The flounder is flat, with both eyes on one side of his body. As for the lobster, he is easily seen and caught. No matter where he hides, his long antennas stick out and show his hiding place. As they say in Kapingamarangi, "That's the end of the story; just a tale told by the people."

The Greedy Boy and the Coconut Crab

There was once a naughty, greedy boy who lived in Thouhou Island, in Kapingamarangi Atoll, in the Eastern Caroline Islands. He loved to eat, and he thought only of himself. He liked to steal food from others. He hoped that it would never be found out.

11

For a long time, he succeeded very well. No one knew that he was a thief. But one of his tricks was discovered, and he was punished. It came about in this way.

A man and his wife found a coconut crab at Paewere, on the eastern side of Thouhou Island. They were poor, and they didn't often have coconut crab to eat, so they felt quite happy.

"Let's cook it and eat it," said the man.

"It's too small," replied his wife. "Let's keep it and feed it until it's much larger."

They left the crab in a deep hole and covered the top, so that it couldn't get out. Then, for many days, they carried food to it. They brought coconut meat and cooked *puraka*, or taro.

The coconut crab lives among coconut trees and grows to large size by stuffing itself with coconut meat. It is a land crab with strong, sharp, cutting claws. Since its main food is coconut, it is delicious to eat.

The man and his wife hoped to eat the crab, when it should become large and fat. But one day, the greedy boy found out about the crab. When no one was around, he stole it, roasted it, and ate it. He had the crab feast all by himself. How he enjoyed that meat! Not once did he think of the people who had fattened the crab for their own use, except to hide from them.

Now the boy didn't want the man and his wife to know that the crab was gone. He wanted them to keep on bringing food to the crab's hole. And who would be there to eat it? He, himself, of course.

"I'm very clever," he said to himself. "I'll just crawl into that hole a couple of times a day and eat up the good food."

That was exactly what he did. Day after day, he stuffed himself with the food intended for the crab. He was down in the hole one day, when the man and the woman came, and he heard them talking together.

"I haven't seen the crab for some time," said the man. "It stays far down in the hole."

"Let's kill it and eat it now," said the woman. "It must be full-grown and fat, by this time."

"Good! We will each make a torch and smoke it out," said the man. So the two went away and tied torches of dry coconut leaves.

The boy wanted them to keep on bringing food, and he thought of a plan. He filled two coconut shells with water and took them into the hole with him.

But the man and woman brought *three* coconut-leaf torches, instead of two. The boy didn't know that. They set fire to one of the torches. When it flamed well, they put it into the hole. The boy took up one shell, threw the water over the torch, and put out the fire.

Then the man and woman set fire to the second torch and put it into the hole. The same thing happened. The boy put out the fire with water from the second shell.

"That's the end of the torches," thought the boy. But he was mistaken. The man and his wife set fire to the third torch. "This will smoke out the crab," they said.

They pushed the torch far down into the hole and moved it all about. Suddenly, they heard someone yelling.

"Ouch! Stop burning me! Stop, stop!" howled the boy.

He crawled out and stood before them. The skin of his body. the hair of his head, and even his eyebrows were burned. The selfish boy suffered a great deal from the burns. But he had to suffer still more when he went about the village. The people pointed him out as the boy who stole food from others. As they say in Kapingamarangi, "That's the end of the story; just a tale told by the people."

The Fight Between the Octopus and the Whale

A long time ago, in the ocean near Yap, an octopus saw whale and swam along beside him. That made the whale angry.

"Why don't you show me respect?" he roared. "Why do you swim along with me? You're only an octopus. I'm a whale, the king of the sea. You ought to swim behind me!"

The octopus swam along as before. "I'm as important as you are," he said. "All the fish of the sea are afraid of me."

"Is that so!" exclaimed the whale. "Well, I'm not afraid of anything that swims in the ocean, not even you!"

They kept on quarreling. At last, the octopus said, "To settle this, let's have a fight and see who is stronger. You name the day."

"Three months from today!" said the whale. "I'll send you word by my messenger fish, when I'm ready."

"Very well," said the octopus, and he swam away.

The whale did nothing to get ready for the fight, except to eat a great deal and grow larger. But the octopus was busy. He took from the bottom of the sea the blackest mud that he could find. He kept it in his body, even in his eyes, his ears, and his nose. Then, one day, the messenger fish came and told him that the whale would fight him the next day.

"I'm ready," said the octopus.

The next day, the octopus saw the whale, who was making a great deal of noise, spouting up air and water high into the sky.

"I'll tease him first," said the octopus. He called out, "Oh, here you come, and I'm so frightened! I'm only a little girl octopus, who can't fight very well. I'm afraid, oh, so afraid of you!"

15

In that way, he got the whale to come close to him. The whale was so sure of winning the fight that he was easily fooled.

Suddenly, the octopus squirted out some of the black mud that he had in his body. He squirted it into the water, which turned black. The whale could no longer see his enemy. They had a big fight. They pushed up waves, mountain high.

The whale hit at the octopus with his head. He struck at him with his front flippers. He swung his tail high up in the air and then smacked it down hard on the water. But where was the octopus? The whale couldn't see him. He smacked and whacked and hit only the sea. The octopus moved around very fast and kept out of the way, squirting the black fluid all the time.

When all the water around the whale was quite black, the octopus swam up to his enemy. He put his long, strong tentacles around the whale's great body, around his flippers and tail, his ears, his eyes, his mouth—wherever he could get a good hold.

The whale fought fiercely. He smacked down his heavy tail, but he could not shake off his enemy. The octopus held him tightly. Then he pushed the whale against a large rock in the ocean and held him there. He squeezed until the whale was dead.

"This will show who is king of the sea," he said.

From that day, the octopus has black fluid always ready for a fight. But nobody calls him the "king of the sea," for he doesn't look or act like a king. He is known as the "pirate of the sea," and that is entirely different.

The Turtles and the Mountain Tunnel

During the second world war, hundreds of caves were dug in the cliffs and mountains of the Pacific Islands. To these, the people went for safety. Sometimes, they had to live in the caves for a long time. But the people of the village of Pata, on Tol Island, in the Truk Atoll, did not need to dig caves. They already had a deep tunnel in which they could hide, if war came their way.

The tunnel reaches from one side of a high mountain to the other, and it has been there for a long time. An old legend tells how it came there.

Tol Island had five small villages. They were all under the rule of a chief named Samoniong. He ruled wisely, and the people were glad to obey him.

The people used to bring their chief the first fruits and vegetables of their trees and gardens. They took pride in doing it. Each of the five villages tried to bring the best foods. In the Pacific Islands, food was always the most valuable gift. The island atolls lay far apart, with the wide ocean between. Food was not always easy to get, or to carry to other places.

Everybody in the village of Pata brought food to the chief at the same time. They held a celebration, with singing, dancing, and a feast. The chief took certain foods for himself. He divided the rest among the people, to be eaten at the feast or taken back home with them. It was a happy time of good will for the whole community.

17

One fine summer day, the people of Pata village prepared a great pile of fruits and other foods. They filled large woven baskets with green drinking coconuts and cooking and eating coconuts. They dug up the largest taros and yams. They picked from the trees the finest breadfruit, papayas, mangos, and other fruits. They brought pigs, chickens, lobsters, coconut crabs, shrimps, and fish for the feast. Even the old men and women helped to carry baskets filled with fruits, vegetables, and cooked foods wrapped in leaves.

The people wore their best clothes, with strings of shells or flowers around their necks and arms, and flowers in their hair.

There were more than a hundred people. They started out on the long way to Samoniong's house, laughing and happy. They walked along the beach. The chief's house and land lay some distance away, on the other side of the island.

Between the village of Pata and the chief's home, there was a high mountain. The people had to walk around it on their way. That part of Tol Island was called Wonei.

A strong, ugly giant named Oneniap had come to live on that mountain. None of the people, not even the chief, knew that he was there. He got his food by stealing.

The people came shouting, singing, and laughing on their way. They carried the heavy loads of food in baskets hung on poles over their shoulders. The giant heard them, as they passed the mountain at Wonei.

"Aha! This is my chance!" he said to himself, as he looked down over the edge of the mountain cliff.

He sprang from the mountain top to the beach, sailing through the air. One minute he was on the mountain, and the next minute, there he was, in front of the people, with a huge club.

"Put down the food! Put down the food!" he shouted. The people were frightened. They gave Oneniap everything they were carrying. He picked it up in his long arms and flew back to the mountain top.

The children began to cry. The other people stood there in anger. Gone were the beautiful fruits and vegetables and everything else. There was nothing for the people of Pata village to do but go home with empty hands.

18

Some of the men went to Chief Samoniong and told him what had happened. The good chief worried about his people. What would become of them now? Such a giant would find a way to eat up everything on Tol Island.

The following night, Samoniong couldn't sleep for worry. He lay on mats in his house and wondered what to do. All of a sudden, he heard a soft voice near the doorway, calling, "Samoniong! Samoniong!"

He got up. There, in the clear moonlight, he saw two large turtles. "Samoniong, why do you worry? We're going to help you," said the first turtle.

Then the second turtle spoke. "We'll make a new road for your people to come to you," it said. "Go to sleep and rest now. You'll see the road in the morning."

The two turtles crawled away in the moonlight. Samoniong went back to his mats and slept. The turtles went to the mountain and began to cut a great hole through it. One turtle worked on each side. They met in the center.

In the morning, when the sun arose, there was a great tunnel, all complete. It reached from Pata village to the home of the chief, on the other side of the island. The turtles were nowhere to be seen.

The people were happy. "We won't have to go around the mountain to get to our chief!" they shouted to each other. "Look, look! We can go right through to the other side!"

They took fruits and other food and went to visit Samoniong. They sang and shouted and laughed, as they entered the tunnel and passed through the mountain. The giant Oneniap heard the sound. He couldn't see anyone, no matter where he looked, because the people were all in the tunnel.

The kind old chief, Samoniong, was delighted. He stood at the far end of the tunnel. He heard the people as they came singing, and he met them with joy. They all went to his house and had a celebration.

Never again did Oneniap trouble the people. They used their tunnel when going from Pata village to the other side of Tol Island, and they are still using it today. In Pata village, the turtle has been much respected ever since.

The Battle of the Birds and the Fish

Once upon a time, in the Eastern Caroline Islands, a great battle was planned between the birds and the fish. Leaders on both sides sent out word that no bird or fish would be excused from taking part. Sea birds, land birds, large birds, tiny birds, all must fight. Also, the fish were ordered to come—the sharks, the bonitos, the beautiful butterfly fishes, and hundreds of others, even the little minnows. The whale and the giant octopus were called and also the crabs, clams, squids and eels.

Some of the birds and fish were upset when they heard about the war. They flew around and swam around in great excitement.

"What's the reason for this war?" asked a small fish.

"War doesn't need any reason, stupid," answered a large one. "We just fight, that's all."

"Why do *I* have to fight?" asked a little land bird. "I'm very busy with my young ones. I have to find food for my family. I have no time to fight fish. I don't even know them! I never go near the reef."

"That doesn't matter," said the large, dark frigate bird. He had a sharp beak that could rip open a fish in one stroke.

"But my little wife and children might starve, if I die in battle," said the bird.

"When leaders say 'fight,' we fight. Isn't that reason enough?" said another bird.

"No," said the little bird, in a weak voice.

"You'll fight, just the same!" said still another bird.

The talk went around among the large, important birds, that whenever there was a war, it was because somebody was hungry.

"Hungry for what?" asked a small bird.

"Oh, this and that. Just hungry."

"How hungry?"

"Hungry enough to take by force from others," was the reply. And that really was the reason for the great battle.

The sea birds and the fish always hunted for food in the lagoon and on the great reef. They liked to eat small fish, crabs, clams, and squid. Birds and fish hunted for food all the time. Sometimes they quarreled. The fish would swim around and chase smaller fish into a pool among the coral rocks. That gave the birds a chance to fly down and steal them. Then again, a bird would dive into the water and snatch up a fine fish or squid. He would fly up into the air with it. If he dropped it, a fish would snap it up and swallow it.

The fight for food had been going on among birds and fish for a long time. One day, a few birds carried some broken coconuts to the reef. They were pecking out the oily food, when a wave carried the coconuts into the water. A school of hungry fish stole the coconuts and carried them away. That was the real cause of the war.

The day came to start the battle. The birds flew down to the reef in armies so large that they darkened the sky. The fish came by thousands. The two armies fought each other fiercely along the shore, in the lagoon, and on the reef. They fought for many days.

The birds dragged the fish out of the water and pecked them to pieces, or left them to die upon the shore. The fish sprang out of the water, grasped the legs or wings of the birds and bit them or pulled them under water. Heads and tails, wings and fins covered the rocks of the reef. The cries of the birds and the sounds of gasping fish filled the air.

It was a terrible war, with many killed on both sides. Some fighters were not certain who their enemies were. Birds killed birds, and fish killed fish. So it was with the whale and the giant octopus. They were so large that they fought by themselves in the deep ocean outside the reef. Neither one knew what the war was about, but they fought for hours and hours.

They made the water fly mountain high. Sometimes the octopus wrapped his long legs and arms around the body of the whale and squeezed him. Then he pulled him under, held him there, and tried to drown him, for the whale had to come up for air once in a while. Then the whale would get loose and strike the octopus with his powerful tail.

The whale and the octopus fought for a long time, before they found out that they were on the same side in the war. Then they swam away, feeling foolish. They didn't even wait to find out which side won the war.

In the lagoon and on the reef were many fights. The birds

took a fish out of the water. They pecked at him and cut him down on all sides, until he became four-cornered, or square. He got away from them finally, but he remained square-cornered. He has been called the "trunkfish" ever since, because of his shape.

Another group of birds took another fish and split him in two, so that he was flat and thin. Then they jumped up and down upon him and made him flat. He was so flat that there wasn't room for both of his eyes. One eye had to go to the top of his head. Then he had two eyes on the same side of his head. He was the flounder. He got away from the birds, but he remained in that shape forever after.

Some of the larger fish had a good time eating the birds and fish that were killed. The shark was one of them. He swam around, snatching and swallowing, snatching and swallowing.

"It's wonderful to have so much food, all at one time!" he said to himself.

No bird would fight him, for he had a large mouth, with sharp teeth. So the larger birds attacked him all together. They picked up heavy stones and dropped them into his face. The shark's lower jaw was pushed out of shape, and he had to stop fighting. His mouth has been out of line ever since that great battle.

Smaller fighters also had some fierce fights. The ray fish heard that the crab was fighting with the birds against the fish.

"That's not fair!" he cried. "You're a fish, like the rest of us!"

"No I'm not. I'm a land animal," said the crab.

At that time, the ray fish had no stinger in his tail, but he carried a large, sharp spine to battle. He became so angry that he swam over and stuck the spine into the face of the crab. The crab became angry. He pushed the sharp stinger very hard into the back of the ray fish, near the end of his tail. The ray fish carries the spine in that place to this very day.

The bird army nearly always had the best of the fight. They could fly and dive, strike the fish, and fly away again. The fish couldn't leap up very high to catch the birds. However, some of the fish made up for it in brave fighting.

One of the leaders of the fish was the sea urchin. He carried a great many spears and, small as he was, he was very brave.

22

Again and again, he fought alone, when other fish swam away in fear. The birds couldn't do a thing with him. Every time they dashed at him, he pricked them sharply, and they flew away.

Many sea turtles moved about. They were not hurt by the pecking of the birds, and small fish hid under their shells.

On a high cliff over the lagoon lived a large bird, the eagle. He had often heard of a sea animal called the *likamantantar*.

"I'll fight that fish!" he screamed. "I don't care to waste my time fighting just anybody. But a sea animal with such a long name must be important, like myself. I'll fiight him and kill him!"

He didn't know that the *likamantantar* was only a simple cocklefish clam, that clung tightly to rocks in the sea.

The eagle spread his great wide wings and flew grandly down to fight. He called out loudly, "Watch me, watch me! Watch me finish the *likamantantar!*"

He flew down to a rock. He looked all around to find the large fish. He didn't notice a female cocklefish clam on the rock. He stood there and stamped his feet upon the rock, flapping his wings and crowing, like a proud rooster longing to fight. All of a sudden, he put both of his feet into the mouth of the clam. She closed her jaws tightly and pinched his legs.

"Ouch, ouch!" screamed the eagle. "Let me go, you silly clam! Let me go! You're not fighting fair!"

She held on tighter. Then his great courage left him, and he fought to get loose. He yelled louder and louder, "Let me go, cockleshell, let me go! I've got to fight the *likamantantar!* Ouch, ouch! You're pinching me! You're pinching me!"

He screamed loudly. He struggled long on the rock and became tired. His cries became weaker and weaker. At last, he begged the clam to let him go, but she hung on tighter than ever.

Then the eagle thought of a plan to fool her and get away. He pretended to be dead. He spread out his wings, dropped his body down upon the rock and lay very still. By and by, the cocklefish opened her jaws very slowly, to see what had happened. The eagle pulled himself free. He sprang into the air and flew away, screaming, "I fooled you, cocklefish, I fooled you!"

He flew around, looking for the *likamantantar.* When the fighting was over, he found out that he had been held fast by the very enemy he tried to find. He knew then that the *likamantantar* was only a clam.

The great battle came to an end at last. Then it was time to count the dead, the wounded, and the living. The fish discovered that the fishes who had stolen the coconuts from the birds hadn't fought at all!

The fish who had fought were angry. "You were the cause of the trouble. You stole the coconuts! Why didn't you help us fight the birds?" they asked.

"We didn't know a thing about the battle," said the fish. "We hid under some stones. We slept all through the war."

The other fish called them cowards. They were ashamed of themselves and tried to hide where they wouldn't be seen. The other fish drove them away. "Don't ever come near us again!" they said.

The coward fish ran away to the places where mangrove bushes grew in shallow water near the shore. There they hid among rocks and roots, and there they are, by themselves, to this day. They are the speckled fish called "sea trout." People fish for them among the mangroves, and they are shy and ashamed, even now.

When the birds flew home from the war, they found out that a certain flying animal had not taken part in the fight. They looked for him and found him on top of a high tree. They surrounded him and drove him down. Then they all gathered around in a circle, with him in the center.

"Why didn't *you* show your face?" they asked. "We didn't see *you* in the fight!"

The flying animal replied, "I didn't fight, because I don't belong either with birds or fish. Don't you see that I have the face of a fox, and that I look like an animal, because I have fur and four legs?"

"You were a coward! Well, you can just stay a coward!" said the birds. "Don't ever come near us again. From now on. when you rest, you shall hang upside down from tree branches."

Ever since then, the flying fox, or fruit bat, is afraid of everything, and hangs upside down to rest and sleep. It has a foxlike face, upright ears, four legs, and wings that look like long thin fingers, held together by skin. It keeps out of the way of all other animals. It hides in caves or in the shade of forest trees.

The great battle was over. Some of the birds and fishes were satisfied, because they had fought long and bravely. They talked about their courage, long after the cause of the war had been forgotten.

Nobody knew which side had won, but both sides knew that a great many lives had been lost.

"Was the war worth while?" asked the little songbird who had been made to fight, against his wishes. But no one ever answered him. And the birds and the fishes went on, the same as ever, struggling to find food in the lagoon and on the reef.

The Whale and the Sandpiper

Here is a story from the Marshall Islands.

One day a great *raj*, or whale, said to a little *kirrir*, or sandpiper, "There are many more whales than sandpipers in the world."

"Not at all!" said the sandpiper. "There are many more sandpipers."

"More whales!" said the whale.

"More sandpipers!" said the sandpiper.

They argued a long time about it. Finally, the whale began to sing and chant, sing and chant:

"Bōttōra, bōttōra ū - ū
Bōttōra ū!
Dri batati raj an i juri,
Bōttōra ū, bōttōra ū!"

The chant was, first, some blowing sounds, as he blew water and air high into the sky. Then, the words of the chant called all the whales to come fast, fast through the water.

All the whales came from the east, pushing up high waves. The great *raj* sang again. Then, all the whales came from the west. The great whale kept on singing. Then, all the whales came from the north and south. At last, all the whales of the ocean were there, splashing and blowing, pushing the waters of the ocean up to the sky.

"Do you see?" said the great whale. "I told you there were more whales than sandpipers!"

"Just wait," said the little sandpiper. He began to chant and sing, chant and sing:

"Kirir i e,
    Kirir i e, kōla raj i e
    Ej mōn iō kolo ñe kar jab
    Bwijirokwa eo ke i baj mij oo-oo-oo!"

The chant was, first, some cheeping, chirping sounds. Then
the words called all the sandpipers in the world: "Come quick!
If I didn't have the eagle to protect me, I would be killed. Come,
sandpipers, oo-oo-oo!"

First, all the sandpipers flew in from the east, and their wings
flapped until a high wind was blowing. The little sandpiper kept
on chanting and singing, chanting and singing. Then, all the
sandpipers came from the west, from the north, and the south,
until the whole sky was dark.

"Do you see?" said the little sandpiper. "I told you there
were more sandpipers than whales."

"Just wait," said the great whale. He began to sing and
chant, sing and chant, calling all the sharks in the ocean.

The *bako*, or shark, heard the song. Soon all the sharks came
from the east. The great whale kept on singing and chanting, and
all the sharks came from the west, from the north, and from the
south, until the ocean was covered with their high fin-sails.

"Look, look!" cried the great whale. "There are many more
whales than sandpipers!"

"Just wait," said the little sandpiper. He began to chant and
sing, chant and sing, calling all the cranes in the world.

The *kabaj*, or crane, heard the song. Soon all the cranes
came from the east. Then, they came flying from the west, the
north, and the south, until the noise was like thunder.

"Look, look!" cried the little sandpiper. "There are many more sandpipers than whales."

The great whale and the little sandpiper kept on calling the fish and the birds with their singing. The *bwebwe*, or tuna, heard it. By and by, all the tunas in the world came swimming from the east, the west, the north, and the south. The *kwolej*, or plover, heard the singing, and they came by thousands. Then the great whale called to the *lejabwil*, or bonito, and the little sandpiper called to the *bejwak*, or noddy tern, and they all came by millions.

And so it went, the great whale singing and chanting, and the little sandpiper chanting and singing, until all the fishes and birds in the world were called together. The noise could be heard high in the sky and over all the land and sea. And still, no one knew whether there were more whales than sandpipers in the world, or more sandpipers than whales.

The fish asked the great whale, "What shall we do now?"

"Let's eat up all the land, so that the birds will die," he said. And they began to eat the land.

The birds asked the little sandpiper, "What shall we do now?"

"Let's drink up the whole ocean, so the fish will die," he said. And they began to drink the ocean.

It took much more time to eat the land than to swallow the water. The birds finished first. They drank up the whole ocean. before the fish had a chance to eat much land. Then, with no water to live in, all the fish died. That is, all except the *kiro*. He had a big belly full of water. He could live a whole day on dry land. The *kiro* lay on the dry ocean bottom for a while. Then he spit out the water that he carried. It made a great pool, but not a whole ocean.

The sea birds began to worry, for they ate fish for food. "We need to have fish," they said.

So the birds spit out all the water they had swallowed and made the ocean again. One by one, the fish became alive and swam around, as well as ever. Then all the fish and birds swam and flew back to their homes, in the east, the west, the north, the south. Everything was just the same as before. No one knew whether there were more whales or sandpipers in the world.

The story of the whale and the sandpiper was a favorite sleepy-time chant in the Marshall Islands. It was sung about many birds and many fish. The chants of the whale and the sandpiper were sung each time a new fish or bird was named.

Like children everywhere, Marshallese boys and girls never wanted to go to sleep at night. They liked to stay awake. They liked to be with older people, listening to them, especially if there were visitors. Marshallese people visited a great deal in the cool evening, after a day of hard work in the sun.

Around an outdoor fire, under the moon and stars, fathers and mothers and older children sat with their friends, talking and laughing. The babies slept. A little distance away, the grandfather or grandmother spread a mat upon the coral stones and called together the children who were too young to stay up late.

Sometimes, the grandmother lay down upon the mat, with the smallest child close to her and the other children near by. She chanted the story of the whale and the sandpiper, over and over. It made the little ones drowsy, and soon, their minds and bodies went to sleep.

The grandmother stopped, now and then, to see if the children were asleep. "What! Not yet?" she would say, as she saw some wide-open eyes. Then she chanted again. Sometimes, it was the grandfather who tended the children and sang.

No child ever heard the story to the end. First, the youngest went to sleep, and then the others, one by one. Their father or grandfather carried them inside the house and put them down upon sleeping mats.

Next day, the children would ask the grandmother, "What happened in the story, after we fell asleep?"

"I'm busy. Wait until this evening," the grandmother said.

Daytime was for work, of which there was a great deal. If a person had a little time free from work in the daytime, he had a nap. The weather was much too warm for storytelling by day. Some people said that it was bad luck to tell stories or sing songs by daylight. "Your head will swell up very large, if you do," said some of the old people, and some of the youngest children believed it.

Stories About Girls and Boys

Children in Micronesia had a good time when they were young. They ran about and played. In the warm climate, they wore little or no clothing. They ate and slept whenever they pleased. Everybody helped to amuse or take care of the youngest ones.

There were no poisonous snakes, insects, or harmful animals in the islands. Only the deep sea was dangerous, with sea animals that could hurt people. In legends, a good child had little to fear, for good young children had a special mana, or magic power, all their own.

Many legends were told about young children. A favorite kind of hero was a superchild who had come to earth in a magical way. He did great deeds while still very young. Some child heroes were brave and industrious and knew how to use magic. Sometimes, a girl or boy hero played a trick on a stupid ghost. In some legends, when a naughty child disobeyed, he was punished.

Some stories were told to children to teach them to be brave, to obey, and to do right instead of wrong. Many of the old legends taught them to respect their elders, the ruling clan and family, and the ancestor gods.

Here are some legends about boys and girls.

Sirene, the Mermaid

Once upon a time, long ago in Guam Island, there was a young girl named Sirene. She was beautiful, sweet, and kind, but there was a strange thing about her. She would go swimming whenever she liked, even if her mother forbade her. She just had to be in the water.

And how she could swim! No other person in all Guam Island could move so fast through the water or stay under so long. She and her mother lived near Agaña Spring, a deep pool in a river that ran past their thatched hut. Sirene was in and out of the pool all day long.

Her mother worked hard, doing housework and gardening. She couldn't understand why Sirene swam so much. Many times a day, she called the child to come and help with the work. Sometimes, Sirene would answer from the river, but often, she was too far down in the water to hear.

"It's time you learned to do something," her mother said, again and again. "Now stay right here and help me."

She tried to teach her daughter to prepare food and cook it; to sweep fallen leaves from the house; to brush the ground with a broom; and to make clothes. But when she turned her back, Sirene ran away again to the river to dive and swim.

At that time, many of the Chamorro people of Guam Island were Christians. Sirene was a Christian girl. She had been baptized, and so she had a *matlina*, or godmother, as well as a mother. The *matlina* was a good woman who loved Sirene very much, no matter how she behaved.

The godmother thought a great deal about the life and happiness of her godchild. "Sirene is my daughter too," she said.

One day, the mother called Sirene, but she received no answer. When Sirene finally came, the mother scolded her. "Where have you been all this time?" she asked.

"Oh, just swimming," said Sirene.

"That's all you do, you naughty girl!" said her mother. "Swim, swim, swim! I'm very angry with you. I hope that soon, very soon, you will turn into a fish. Then you can swim all the time."

In that way, the mother put a curse upon her daughter. Suddenly, there stood the godmother, who always came when Sirene was in trouble.

"I heard the curse you placed upon Sirene, wishing that she would turn into a fish," she said. "I can't let you have that wish. I have helped to christen this child, Sirene. She is part mine, and I won't have her turned into a fish."

The mother was frightened at what she had done. "Oh, save her, save her!" she cried.

"It's too late for me to save her entirely," said the godmother. "You, her mother, have already spoken the curse. Half

of her body will remain as I wish, for I am her *matlina*. But the curse will fall upon the other half."

The godmother chose the upper part of the young girl's body as her own. "When I christened you, my child," she said, "I christened your heart, your mind, and your thoughts. They are in the upper part of your body. That shall stay as it is. Your mother's curse will change only the lower half."

Then the godmother spoke magical words, so that only half of Sirene's body would be changed.

Before the mother could say another word, Sirene ran away to the river. She jumped in, and the lower part of her body changed into that of a fish. She was happy. She could swim much faster and stay under water longer. She dived and played in the water. Then away she swam to the ocean, a silvery mermaid, going through the water like lightning.

She was seen, here and there, along the way. She swam from

Agaña Spring in the *minondo*, the deepest part of the river, to Agaña Bay and the blue Pacific Ocean.

Her mother and her godmother never saw her again, but Guamanian fishermen often have seen her or heard her. She dives and swims as she pleases, and sometimes she rests near shore, singing and singing.

And what does she sing? Ah, you must ask the fishermen. They can tell you.

The Story of a Good Boy

There was once a boy in the Eastern Caroline Islands who loved the sea so much that he was nearly always out fishing. One day, as he went home, he found a large fish. It had flopped over upon dry rocks and was suffering. The boy felt sorry for the fish. He laid it carefully back in the water.

The fish looked up and said to him, "Take one of my scales. If you want to go under water, this scale will lead you safely wherever you wish. Just ask it to take you."

The boy took a scale from the fish and kept it. Then he went back to the village. The chief of the island was holding a meeting. The chief said to the people, "My wife has disappeared in the sea. Someone has stolen her. Whoever finds her and brings her back will get a reward. Who will go?"

The people were silent. They had heard that at the bottom of the sea, there was one of the heavens where ghosts and spirits live. It was a lovely place, but human beings couldn't go there alone without becoming lost or drowning. Sea spirits sometimes stole human beings and took them to the undersea paradise to live with them. That had happened to the chief's wife, and he wanted her back.

At last the boy spoke. "I'm willing to try," he said.

"Go, then!" cried the chief.

The boy went to the reef, carrying the fish scale with him. He dived into the deep water near the place where the woman had last been seen.

33

"Lead me to the place where she is now," he said.

The scale took him far under water. There he saw the under
sea paradise. There were sea animals, sea spirits, and sea ghosts.
There were coral-rock houses and many trees and flowers. With
the fish scale in his hand, he wandered over the place. He went
from one fish and sea spirit to another, but he didn't find the
missing woman. Finally, he came to a large *malekelek* fish, and
there she was.

"I'll take you safely home again," the boy said to her. "Put
your scarf over the *malekelek*, so he won't know you're leaving."

The woman did so. The boy led her away from the undersea
heaven to the top of the ocean and to her home. The chief was
happy to see her, and the boy was given many gifts.

One day, when he was walking to the shore to go fishing, he
found a bird. It was tangled in some coconut-husk twine that had
been dropped in the path. The bird cried, "Don't kill me! Set
me free!"

The boy bent down, freed the bird, and let it go. It flew to a
near-by branch and said to him, "Pull a feather from my wing and
keep it. If you wish to fly somewhere, just ask the feather to take
you."

34

The boy took a feather and kept it.

Soon after that, the chief's wife became very ill. Nothing could save her but some heavenly life-water. It would bring life to those who were dead or dying, and it could be found only in heaven.

The chief called his people together and said, "Whoever can bring my poor wife some of the heavenly life-water shall be chief in my place and rule all the land."

The people shook their heads. "We can't get it," they said. "We cannot fly to heaven."

Then the boy thought of the bird's feather, and said, "I'll try."

"Go then," said the chief.

The boy took the feather and also a little taro leaf. Suddenly the bird came and stuck the feather to the boy's arm. He flew high up to heaven. There he found a clear pool of fresh water. He took up some of it in the little taro leaf and carried it away carefully.

He flew down to earth. He brought the life-water to the chief's wife, and she became well again. The chief kept his promise, and the boy became ruler.

Tik and Lap and the Giant Fish

In some Pacific Islands, it is the custom for the people to give presents to each other, and also to strangers. They give willingly. Nothing makes them happier than to be able to give. They bring gifts with smiles.

It also is the custom that giving should bring return gifts. When children are growing up, their parents teach them not to take gifts, unless they can give something or do something in return. They are taught to respect gifts of food, for food is valuable in the islands. Food is sometimes scarce. The people must live on what their islands produce. In olden days, there were no boats bringing supplies. Food was the best gift, the greatest gift.

An old legend of Ponape tells about two boys who tried to make a return gift of food.

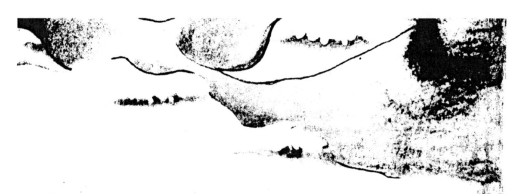

Once, there was a good woman in Ponape who had twin sons. Their names were Ninuau Tik and Ninuau Lap, but they were sometimes called "Tik" and "Lap." They were clever boys. They were small in size, but both of them knew how to use magic.

Tik and Lap were still quite young, but they loved the sea and were good fishermen. They made sharp spears out of hard wood. They dived and speared fish for a living for themselves and their mother. She was proud of her sons, but she was worried about them.

"Every time you go out and dive in deep water to spear fish," she said, "I'm afraid I'll never see my boys again."

"Oh, mother, we can take care of ourselves," said Tik.

"We can swim and dive and use our spears," said Lap.

"If only I could be sure of that!" she said. "But that ocean —ah, it's no friend, that ocean, even though it gives us good food. It lies there, waiting to snatch."

The boys said no more. But they felt sure that they were more clever than the ocean and everything in it.

Tik and Lap loved to be near the water. They longed to have a canoe and sail over the waves. But in the water lay danger and death. Fierce sea animals were there, ready to attack. A couple of boys like Tik and Lap would have made a good meal for some of them.

Since their mother worried about them, Tik and Lap went to fish in places farther away. They looked carefully before they dived to spear a fish under water.

"Nothing can ever catch me," said Tik.

"Nor me," said Lap.

One day, they went to a reef in front of an island called Samuin. They saw smoke above the trees on shore.

"Someone is cooking food," said Tik.

"Let's go ashore," said Lap.

When they went ashore, they saw a great many people, who were having a feast for their chief. They had brought food enough for many people. They saw the two young lads standing there. "Come and welcome," they said.

The boys had a good time that day. When they were ready to leave, the chief gave them gifts of food to take home. There was too much to carry, so the chief gave them a canoe in which to load the gifts. The boys thanked the Chief and sailed home.

"Where did you get the canoe and all that food?" asked their mother.

"The chief of Samuin Island gave it to us," they replied. They told her about the feast.

"Gifts must be paid for," said the mother. "You must go out early tomorrow morning and catch fish. Take them all to the chief. But now that you have a canoe, you will go to deeper waters than ever. Oh, do be careful, my sons!"

"We're much more clever than the fish and the storms and waves," said the boys.

"No one is so clever as that," said their mother. "I'm afraid that you'll be careless."

The boys went out very early the next morning to fish for the chief. They took along a large coconut to eat. They also took along some pieces of wood for a fire, so that they could roast it.

They fished all morning. Then they went ashore on rocky land that reached out into the water. Tik cracked the coconut in two. Lap started to make a fire. One half of the coconut fell into the water, which was very deep at that place.

The two boys dived at the same time. They wanted to get it back, for they had no other food. They forgot, just that one time, to look before they dived.

At that place, there was a giant fish. He saw the two diving bodies in the water. He opened his wide mouth. One swallow was enough for both. Down, down they slid, inside the fish, and then they came to a stop.

"We weren't so clever," said Tik.

"We know that now," said Lap.

They moved about in the dark. "We're in its stomach," said Tik.

"Let's make a fire," answered Lap.

He was still holding the two pieces of wood. They rubbed the wood and made a fire. It lighted the inside of the fish's stomach. The boys held the ends of the wood.

The fish felt the fire and gave a great jump in the sea. The fire became hotter and hotter, as the wood burned. The fish swam about, in and out among the coral rocks, up and down in the water. Finally it swam far, far out to sea. Then it dived deeply and rolled around at the bottom of the ocean.

At last, it came to the top of the water, dead. The waves carried it upon the beach of Samuin Island. The boys crawled out quickly.

"We've had a long ride," said Tik.

"And we've caught a fish," said Lap.

They went to the chief of Samuin Island. "We have a fish that is too large for us to carry," said Tik. "Will you please take it as a gift?" said Lap.

The chief thanked the boys. He and his people went down to the shore. They were surprised when they saw what was there. They never before had seen such a large fish.

"You boys are so short and small," the chief said. "How could you catch such a fish? What bait did you use?"

"We were the bait," said Tik. "The fish swallowed us."

"He had a stomach-ache, and he died of it," said Tik.

"You are clever boys, and you will be wise men," said the chief.

Tik and Lap left the place and sailed back to their mother. They told her about their fish.

"I wanted you to catch fish for the chief," she said, "but not exactly in that way."

"We were careless," said the boys.

"You have learned your lesson," said their mother. From that time, she did not worry about her sons.

"You are quite able to take care of yourselves," she said.

The Children and the Ghost-Woman

Once upon a time, in the Eastern Caroline Islands, a woman had four children, three girls and a boy. All of them were small and young. The boy, Limas-amaskapuer, was the smallest and youngest of all. They were good children, but sometimes they forgot what their mother had told them. They just forgot.

One day, the children went walking together, much farther than their mother wanted them to go. They wandered until they were tired. At last, they came to a house in the forest.

"Perhaps we could go there and rest," said one of the children.

Now it happened that a ghost-woman lived there. She looked like a woman, but she was half woman and half ghost. The ghost-woman was wicked. She sometimes ate people, but the little children didn't know that.

She saw the three small girls and the tiny boy standing in the path. She called to them in a sweet voice, "Come to me, my pretty little ones."

The children did not go at once. She was so ugly that she frightened them. Then she lied to them. "Don't you know me?" she asked. "I'm your relative, your ancestor. We are of the same family and clan."

"Oh," said the children to each other, "she's one of our family. She will be kind to us." So they went to her.

"Come into the house, my beautiful children," she said. "I love you."

She did indeed love little children, if she could get them to eat. The children went into the house with her. They were so tired that they lay down upon the floor and went to sleep.

When the ghost-woman saw that they were asleep, she was happy. She stooped over and poked each one of them with a long, thin finger.

"They feel cold," she said. "I'll warm them up a little."

She took some sleeping mats and rolled them around the three little girls. She tied the roll with rope.

"Now you can't get out, my dears!" she said.

There wasn't room for the small boy in the mats. She lifted

40

him up and carried him over near the stone oven to warm. She
covered him with large dry leaves from a basket. Then she went
outside and pushed some heavy rocks against the door.

"They can't get out, they can't get out," she said to herself.

She intended to eat the children. "Let them warm, let them
warm," she sang.

She took up a clamshell knife and went over to a large flat
rock that stood a little way from the house. She sat down upon
it and sharpened the knife with a stone. She chanted a song to
the sun god, who was shining high in the sky. Her song went
something like this:

> "Sun, sun, hurry and go down, go down,
> For then I can eat the children.
> And you will not see, oh, you will not see!
> Oh, sun, how I will enjoy
> Eating those dear children!"

She sang the song over and over and louder and louder, while sharpening her clamshell axe. By and by, the noise awoke the little boy, Limas-amaskapuer. The ears of the girls were covered with the heavy sleeping mats, but his were not covered. He lay there and listened to the ghost-woman's song. Then he pushed away the large leaves and got up and listened again.

He looked around the room. There wasn't a place where he could hide. He ran to the door, but he couldn't push it open, because of the rocks against it outside. Then he ran over to his sisters. He pounded the roll of mats with his hands.

"Wake up, wake up!" he called softly.

The girls woke up and tried to push open the roll of mats, but it was tied too well. "We can't open the mats," they said.

"Crawl out at the end, then," whispered the little boy, and so they did.

"Now hear what I hear," he said.

The little girls listened. They heard the ghost-woman outside, singing about eating them. "What shall we do?" they cried.

They ran around the room, trying to find a way to get out. There was a very small hole in the corner of the house that the wind had broken. The children crawled through it, one by one. When all were outside, they ran as fast as they could, toward home.

Just then, the ghost-woman came back into the house. She cut the rope that she had put around the roll of mats, and she said to herself, "Ah, just a little while, just a little while, and they'll be good and warm and ready to eat."

A little green lizard on the wall heard her and said, "Oh, do keep still. They left a long time ago."

"You lie, you do!" cried the ghost-woman. "And just for that, I'll not give you even a tiny taste, when I eat them."

She stepped hard on the roll of mats, to feel if the little girls were still inside, but there was nothing in them. She ran to the pile of dry leaves near the stone oven and kicked them, but she found nothing.

She became very angry. She ran around the house, sniffing in every corner. At last she smelled the way to the place where they had crawled out of the house.

"They got out right here!" she screamed. She went out of the house and ran after them.

"She's coming, she's coming!" the children cried.

By that time, they had reached a little pond. Beside it stood a large breadfruit tree. Its branches hung over the water.

"Let's climb up into the tree," they cried, and up they went, first the three little girls and then the little boy.

Now ghosts are clever in some ways, but in other ways, they are often foolish. So it was with the ghost-woman. The children sat in the tree, but did she think to look up there? Not she! She ran up and down the road for a while, sniffing and sniffing. She could smell that they had gone no farther than the pool. She ran all around it, but she couldn't find the children. They sat very still, clinging to a large branch.

Then the ghost-woman looked down in the water, and she saw the picture of the four children on top of the water. "Aha, there you are!" she said. She thought that the children were in the pool.

She jumped into the deep water, swishing here, swashing there, groping in the water with her long arms. She swam and she dived, and she swam and she dived, and she swam so long that she nearly was drowned. Then she came up again. She clambered to the edge of the pond and sat there choking for air. She made such funny faces that the children in the tree laughed aloud. Then she found out where they were. She reached up her long arms.

"Come down, my dear, dear, little children. Come down to me!" she called.

"No, no! You climb up to us," the children said.

She started to climb the big tree. It was hard work for her, but up she came. At last, she nearly reached the foot of the little boy with her fingers.

"Come, my pretty one, come!" she said, but he pulled up his foot. Then the children began to sing:
"Climb up, climb up,
Climb up and over,
Up and over, up and over!
I hope you'll make a wrong step, a wrong step,
And skin off some of your skin!"

The ghost-woman's foot slipped, and she fell crashing down and skinned her front. She howled. "Now how shall I come up there, with my front all skinned?" she cried.

"Climb up backwards, stupidhead, climb up backwards, stupidhead," chanted the children.

And the silly ghost-woman did so. Or, at least, she tried. She climbed backwards until she was near the small boy again, and the children kept on chanting:

"Climb up, climb up,
Climb up and over,
Up and over, up and over!
I hope you'll make a wrong step, a wrong step,
And skin off some of your skin!"

The ghost-woman fell crashing down, backwards. That time, she skinned her back. "What shall I do now?" she screamed. "Both my front and my back are scratched and skinned!"

The children called to her, "Rub yourself with ashes! Then go jump into the salt water!"

The ghost-woman rubbed herself all over with ashes. It stung, and she howled. Then she ran down to the shore and jumped into the salt water. That stung her too. She dived into the deep water until she drowned.

The four little children got down from the tree and ran home to their mother. It was the first time they had ever gone far in the forest by themselves. And it was the last time. The very last time!

The Two Brothers and the Ghost Mo'oi

A story told in Yap is about two brothers. They both were fine-looking boys, with handsome faces and thick curly hair held in place with high wooden combs. But the two brothers were alike only in looks. The elder one, a Fisherboy, was industrious. He always went fishing to get food for the family. But the younger brother, a Lazyboy, never wanted to go along. He only wanted to play tricks. He caught mice and killed them just for fun.

One day, the Lazyboy caught mice in a net. After that, he went to steal some fine breadfruit that belonged to a woman named Mo'oi.

Now Mo'oi was really a *kan*, a ghost-woman. She wore a grass skirt and some necklaces of string and shells, like ordinary women. But her eyes had a mean look. She ate people, if she could manage to do so without being found out. The Lazyboy knew it.

"She's half human and half ghost," he said to himself that day, "but I'm far more clever than she. I'll get some of her breadfruit without her seeing me."

The ghost-woman came and stood under the tree, while he was there. He was careless and let a breadfruit fall, and it struck her back.

"Oh, ho," she said, picking it up. "Fruit is falling from my tree already."

She ate half of the breadfruit without cooking it. She put the other half in her basket. The boy moved, in the tree, making a noise. She looked up and saw him.

"*Ei, ei*, you up there!" she called. "What are you doing in my tree? I'm going to eat you, my fine lad!"

Now ghosts are very clever in some ways, but stupid in others, and the Lazyboy was not at all afraid. "I can easily fool her," he said to himself.

He clambered down lower on the tree to a branch that was closer to the ghost-woman. Then he threw her a dead mouse from his net. She reached up and caught it and ate it. Then he threw her a second one, but that one was alive, and it ran away. The ghost-woman went after it, and the boy got down from the tree.

Mo'oi caught the mouse and ate it. Then she came back to get the boy, but he was gone.

The next day, the elder brother, the Fisherboy, went to fish again. Lazyboy stayed at home and caught more mice. Again, he went over to the breadfruit tree. Again, the ghost-woman came. Again, a breadfruit fell down and struck her. She looked up and saw the boy at once.

"I'll get you, this time!" she said.

The Lazyboy clambered down nearer to her and threw mice to her, one after the other, but they were all dead. He gave her all that he had. He felt sure that he could run away from her, and so he sprang down from the tree. But Mo'oi caught him. She put him quickly into her basket, and fastened the cover tight.

She carried him to her house. It was built high on posts. Beneath the bamboo floor, she had several cupboards, where she kept things. In the first one were bones of mice; in the second, bones of cats; in the third, bones of dogs; and in the fourth were human bones. She locked the boy in that cupboard.

When the Fisherboy came home that day, he missed his brother and went looking for him. When he came to Mo'oi's house, he asked, "Where's my brother?"

"I don't know," replied the ghost-woman.

But the Lazyboy called out, "I'm here, I'm here!"

"He was stealing my fruit," screamed Mo'oi, "and now he belongs to me!"

"Ah, so that's it," said the Fisherboy. He knew that the ghost-woman wouldn't open the cupboard and let his brother out, so he began to talk with her.

"What are you most afraid of?" he asked.

"I'm most afraid of a spear, a conch shell, and a *tsagal* belt," she said. "And what are *you* most afraid of, boy?"

"Oh, me?" said the Fisherboy, hoping to fool her. "When I eat cooked fish and toasted taro-cake, I'm frightened."

The Fisherboy ran home. He put on a *tsagal* belt, which had been woven in a magical way. He took up a conch shell and a long wooden spear. Then he ran back to Mo'oi.

A strange fight took place between the Fisherboy and the ghost-woman. The boy pretended that he was going to kill her with his spear. He lifted it high and jabbed the air with it. He plunged toward her and made faces at her. She saw the spear and the *tsagal* belt and threw cooked fish and taro-cake at him. The Fisherboy liked those foods very much. He caught them, ate a few, and put the rest upon the ground.

When Mo'oi had thrown all the fish and taro-cake that she had, the Fisherboy blew the conch shell. That frightened the ghost-woman. She ran away into the brush. She made herself smaller and smaller and changed herself into a coconut crab. She ran quickly into a hole under a tree.

Then the Fisherboy got his younger brother out of the cupboard. The two boys picked up the rest of the fish and taro-cake and took it home with them.

Soon, a heavy rainstorm came and a river of water ran into the crab hole. Mo'oi drowned before she could change herself back into a woman again.

The Naughty Girl and the Ghost-Giant

The name of the girl in this story has been forgotten, and perhaps it is a good thing. Why should anyone remember the name of a bad child? It is enough to remember what happened to her and to her parents.

Long ago, in Kusaie Island, there were a mother and father named Katineap and Soap. They had one child, a daughter. No one in the village liked her, for she was selfish and lazy.

She never obeyed. Whenever her parents asked her to do something, she did just the opposite. She refused to help her mother weed the taro garden. She liked to eat but wouldn't help with the cooking, no, no, no, not she! And she wouldn't tend to the fire. That was too much trouble for her.

She liked to play on the beach and bathe and swim in the water. But she never would carry a little basket and gather shellfish and crabs in the shallow water of the lagoon or the mangrove swamp.

"I don't like such work," she would say. "Mother can do it by herself."

Did she help take care of the small children of her relatives? Never! She was too busy combing her hair. Her father and mother scolded her, but it did no good. She still had her own way.

That went on for a long time, until she was quite a large girl. Finally, Soap said to his wife. "She doesn't know how lucky she is, here with us."

"It would be far better," said Katineap. "if we didn't have her."

"Yes," replied Soap. "If only she would go away!"

Those were cruel words, but the parents did not love their daughter. They wanted her to go away. "But where can she go?" they asked each other. At last, they thought of an island which lay by itself, far away on a distant reef.

"Let's teach her a lesson," said Soap. "Let's put her by herself on that island."

"Yes, yes!" cried Katineap. "Let her make herself a house of coconut leaves. Let her weave mats and clothing for herself.

Let her find breadfruit and coconuts for food. Let her learn to raise taro and catch shellfish and crabs."

One day, they took the girl to ride with them in the outrigger canoe. They sailed to the faraway island and went ashore. When the girl was looking the other way, Katineap and Soap went back to the canoe and paddled away. She saw them go and ran along the shore, crying and calling to them not to leave her. But they went on, without even looking back. She was left by herself.

She did not cry long. Very soon, she wiped her eyes and walked around to see what she could find. Her parents thought that no one lived on the island. Someone did live there—the huge, ugly ghost-giant named Kot. Many island people were afraid of him. He pretended to live like a human being, but he also liked being a ghost, so that he could steal and kill without being seen.

The girl wandered until she came to a large house that stood among the trees. She walked to it and went inside. She saw no one.

A pretty dove sat on a rafter, looking at her. It was the ghost-giant's pet.

"Better not let Kot see you," said the dove.

"Why not?"

"He lives here, and he eats people."

"Where is he?" asked the girl, looking about.

"Out fishing on the reef," said the dove. "He'll be coming back, any minute now."

"Where can I go?" she asked.

"Under the floor boards," said the dove.

The girl squeezed herself under the floor boards and there she lay, hardly daring to move.

When Kot came in from fishing, he took some coconut oil from a coconut-shell dish and rubbed his body with it. He spilled some of it, here and there. A drop of the oil fell between the floor boards and went into the eye of the girl. She tried to wipe it away, and she bumped against the floor planks.

"What's that?" roared Kot. "A ghost or a human being?"

The girl said nothing. Kot pulled up the floor boards and saw her there.

"Aha, a child!" he cried. "If it's a boy, I'll kill him and eat him. If it's a girl, she shall be my daughter!"

He dragged up the child. "Oho, a girl!" he shouted. "Now I shall have someone to work for me."

"I don't like to work," said the girl.

The giant laughed. "Go down to the shore and carry up the fish that I caught," he said.

He gave her a rough push. She had to obey, for she was afraid of him. She went down to the beach and tried to take up the large basket of fish, but she could not. So she went back.

"The basket is too heavy. I can't lift it up," she said.

"Speak to me properly," said Kot. "You go back there. Then you call me and say, 'Papa, I can't raise the basket.'"

She went back and called, "Papa, I can't lift up the fish. They are too big and heavy."

Then Kot was satisfied with his new daughter. He went down to the beach and carried the fish to the house. He sat down and

began to eat them raw, and he threw one to the child. She couldn't eat fish raw, and there was no one but herself to cook it.

"Papa," she said, "make a fire, and I will cook the fish."

But Kot did not know how to make a fire. He ate everything raw, for he was afraid of fire.

The girl went outside and found two sticks and some dry leaves. She had seen her parents make fire, and she remembered how it was done. She rubbed the sticks together until there were sparks, and then she laid the leaves upon them.

When the fire took hold of the leaves, Kot ran away. The girl called, "Papa, come back! The fire isn't bad, it's good. It will make our food better to eat."

So Kot came back and watched. She cooked the fish and breadfruit and gave him some, to taste.

"Ah, how clever my daughter is!" he said, smacking his lips.

He ate a huge meal. The poor girl cooked and cooked and cooked. And she had to get all the wood for the fire, for Kot did nothing but eat.

Afterwards, she ate by herself. Then she had to get dry palm leaves and make a bed for herself in a corner. Kot took all the mats to the platform where he slept.

From that time, the child lived with Kot as his daughter. He made her work from morning until night, so that he could live well, like a human being. She had to plant a taro garden and hoe it and weed it. She had to gather fruits and weave baskets and make clothing for herself and Kot.

The ghost-giant ate enough for at least six persons. She cooked for many hours each day. Young as she was, she had to do the work of several women, all by herself. The only thing Kot did was to fish. The girl had no time left for play.

And was she sorry that she had not been a better girl at home? Indeed not. "My mother and father are to blame for everything," she said to herself.

She worked hard until she grew up to be a young woman. "It's time for me to have a husband," she said to Kot one day.

Kot laughed. "There's no one on the island but you and me," he said. "You'll have to marry me."

So she became Kot's wife, and after a time, she had a child.

Kot was very proud of it. He was more kind to the girl then. And so, for the first time, she asked for something.

"I work too hard," she said. "I need some people here. I want to have someone to wash the child every day and watch him."

Kot went outside and spoke to a banana tree that he had. "Drop down bananas at once," he said, "and let them be changed into helpers for my wife."

Plop, plop, down dropped some bananas to the ground. Up stood five strong women, ready to work for the girl. And was she happy then? Not she! No, indeed.

"I need more people. There is water to get every day," she said.

Kot told some other bananas to fall down, and there stood three more women.

The girl never had to work hard again. That part of her punishment was over. But she had to stay on the island with the ugly ghost-giant.

It happened that her parents, Katineap and Soap, heard that their daughter had a child, who was being raised like a prince.

"If we have a rich grandson, we ought to go and see him," they said. They forgot that they had left their daughter, a long time before.

They got ready, took some other people along, and sailed away to the island. Their daughter was bathing near the shore when the canoe came. She ran to the house, calling, "Kot! Kot!"

"What is it?" he asked.

"My mother and father and some other people are coming," she said. "What shall I do?"

"Go back to the beach," he said. "Call out to them to change into *kiol* fish and *sol* fish."

She ran back to the shore. The canoe had come through the passage in the reef and was nearly at the beach. The people in it called out a greeting to her.

She said, "Be changed into *kiol* fish and *sol* fish!"

Her mother and father and the people with them fell into the water and turned into fish. From that time, they had nothing to eat but the poor scraps of food that she threw into the water.

Even today, in the shallow water along the shore, those small fish can be seen, always hungry and hunting for bits of food.

Stories About Ghosts and Giants

Legends of the island people sometimes told about heaven and heavenly spirits. In some stories, heaven was above the earth, or below the sea, or in a faraway island. Sometimes, in a story, there were several heavens. Some legends told about a person who died. He became a spirit and went to heaven. He lived there almost as he had lived on earth as a human being.

In some stories, the gods in heaven were spirits of men and women who had been leaders of people on earth. If a chief or hero had done great deeds on earth, he usually had many followers and a high place in heaven.

Some legends told about spirits that liked to go back to earth and live among human beings. Sometimes, they were half human and half ghost, and they could change into other forms. There were many legends about ghosts and half-ghosts and their doings on earth and heaven. Some were wicked. They stole. They killed and ate human beings. Other ghosts were good and were liked by the people among whom they lived.

There were stories about demons, giants, and other monsters who were believed to have lived on earth, usually doing harm to people. Sometimes, a great hero would fight and kill such a monster.

Here are some stories about ghosts and giants.

The Greedy Giant and the Palau Islands

There are many islands in the Palau group. They lie together in an odd way. They are something like the parts of a human body that has been broken up—the body of a giant. An old Palauan legend tells the story of the giant.

In Angaur Island, long ago, there was born a child whose parents named him Uwab. He was no different from other children, except that he was very greedy. He ate entirely too much. He grew so fast that it was a surprise to all who saw him.

53

From the very beginning, he ate more each day than his father and mother together. He ate so much that when he was a few years old, he was much larger than either of them. The more food they gathered and cooked for him, the more he wanted, for he was selfish as well as greedy. He became taller and taller and fatter and fatter. He became too large to live in his home. It took many men to build a house large enough for him.

He soon outgrew the house. In no time at all, his head hit the roof. The people had to build him a larger house. He outgrew that one also and had to have another one, still larger.

Like all selfish persons, Uwab had a mean temper. He was always shouting at his poor father and mother to bring him more and more to eat and drink.

At last, they had only a little food left. They went to the chief of Angaur Island and said, "Oh, Chief, we come to you in great trouble. Our son Uwab is growing to be a giant. We can no longer feed him."

"How much does he eat?" asked the chief.

"Every day," they said, "he has to have pork, chicken, fish, crabs, lobsters, wild pigeons, coconuts, taro, bananas, sweet potatoes, pandanus, coco syrup and sugarcane; also, many basins of spring water and coconut milk. He eats and drinks it all and shouts for more. He is very angry when we cannot get it for him. We're afraid of him!"

The chief was surprised. He felt sorry for the parents of such a son. "You shall have help," he said.

He told all the people of Angaur Island to help feed the monster son. Uwab ate and drank everything that the people brought. He had fifty large baskets of food each day and dozens of basins of spring water and coconut milk, but he shouted for still more.

He grew and grew, until he was so fat that he could no longer reach up and feed himself. Other people had to push the food into his mouth. It took a number of strong men to do it. People came from near and far to see it done.

The time came when he was so tall that his mouth was hard to reach. So the people fastened long pieces of bamboo together to make a very long pole. They tied Uwab's food to the end of the pole and fed him in that way. Almost every day, they added another pole.

At last, Uwab became so very fat and tall that nothing in the island could reach his mouth. Then he lay down inside his great house and let the people bring him food and drink. In a short time, he became too large for that house also, and he had to leave one enormous leg outside. Soon the other leg had to stay outside. By and by, both of his arms also were outside.

The people became so frightened that they met secretly in a forest, where Uwab could not hear them. "What are we going to do?" they asked each other. "One of these days, Uwab will break out of his house and walk around the island. All our gardens and food trees will be destroyed. He may harm our children."

They could think of only one plan. "We must kill him," they said. "Let us all attack him together."

"But we can't get near him with clubs and spears," someone said. "He's too dangerous."

"Then let's kill him without being near him," said another. And so it was agreed.

By that time, Uwab was so large that he could keep only his head in the house. The rest of his body lay outside on the beach.

The people made long ropes out of fibers of leaves and bark. They waited until the giant was asleep. Then some of the bravest men climbed up on his house and tied his long hair to the roof. The other people gathered together hundreds of pieces of firewood and piles of dry coconut leaves and husks. They put them around Uwab and his house and built fires.

Uwab could not get away. He roared loudly and he kicked with his legs and feet. He fought so hard that the island of Angaur shook. He died quickly, but his last kicks were so strong that he kicked himself into many pieces, large and small. They scattered far and near and settled into the ocean as islands. Many of the people finally went to live on them.

"We fed Uwab. Now let him feed us," they said.

The Palau Islands remain in the same places today. Uwab's head is one part of the island of Ngerechelong. Some people say that Peleliu is part of his legs, and for that reason, it is rocky and rugged. Others say that his legs, pulled up and kicking, are the high land at Aimeliik. The large island of Babelthuap is the trunk of the giant's body.

The people of Ngiwal, a village on Babelthuap Island, like to tell visitors about their own part of Uwab's body. "We live right in the middle of Uwab's stomach," they say. "That gives us the right to eat seven times a day."

Some Palauans say that the people who live on the part of Uwab that was his mouth, talk too much. Those who live on the part that was his legs, can run very fast. Are those things true? Perhaps the people of Palau can tell.

The Ten Brothers and the Stolen Fish

Once upon a time, a young boy became king. This is how it happened.

The village of Lukaf is in the island of Puluwat, in the Puluwat Atoll. There, long ago, lived ten brothers, whose names were Hak, Diu, Wal, Fu, On, Lim, Fan, Jol. Riu, and Jot. Hak was the eldest, and he was king of the island. Jot, the youngest, was only a boy.

Those ten brothers got along very well, until a certain trouble came to them. A ghost-demon named Ligan lived near them. He stayed at a place called Aredau, in the southern part of the island. Ligan drove away all human beings who came near, or else he ate them up. He took more and more land along the shore. At last, he had most of the good fishing places.

The ten brothers always went fishing together. Each had his own outrigger canoe, and each had his own line and hook. One day, they fished for *toku*, or bonito. They paddled to the deep water near Aredau, which the ghost-demon had taken for himself. It was the only good fishing place for bonito.

Ligan saw them go through the passage of the reef and out into the ocean, but he didn't stop them. "Let them fish in my water," he said to himself. "Let them work—for me!"

So the brothers paddled over the deep waves and threw out their lines. The sun shone brightly, the sky and sea were very blue, and fishing was good. The brothers sang and laughed and shouted to each other.

When the setting sun made the sky and sea red, they paddled toward shore. Hak led the way. The other canoes followed in a long line, one after the other. Hak had caught ten bonitos; Diu had caught nine; Wal had caught eight; and so on, down to young Jot, who had caught only one. Each brother was happy with his catch.

To get home, they had to paddle through the only passage in the reef. There Ligan sat among the rocks. As Hak came in his canoe, the ghost saw him and cried out, "Hak!"

"What!" called Hak.

"Is that you coming now?"

"Yes!"

"Have you caught fish in these waters?"

"Yes, ten large bonito."

"Good! Give them to me at once. If you don't, I'll tear you apart and eat you."

Hak was frightened, and he gave the greedy ghost his ten fine fish. Then he paddled through the passage and went home. The same thing happened to the other brothers, one by one, as they came to the passage. Diu had to give up his nine fish, Wal his eight fish, and so on. Jot, the youngest brother, tried to keep his one fish, but he had to give it to the ghost. The ten boys went home hungry.

One day, not long after Ligan had taken their catch, the brothers tried bonito fishing again. "Maybe we can get our canoes through the passage without being seen," said Hak.

Jot, the youngest, spoke up. "I'm not going today," he said. "I have other things to do."

Jot wasn't afraid of Ligan. He had heard that all ghosts were stupid. "I'm as clever as Ligan," he said to himself.

When his brothers had gone fishing, he took a heavy rope and walked over to Aredau. He climbed up onto the high branch of a large breadfruit tree that stood at the edge of a deep pond near Ligan's house. The branch reached out, over the water.

"Let him come now," said young Jot to himself.

By and by, the ugly ghost, Ligan, came out of the house and leaned over to get a drink. Suddenly, he saw the picture of the boy on the smooth, dark top of the water. He rubbed his hands with joy. "A fine bite for me to swallow!" he said.

He dived into the pool to catch Jot, and he smacked his head hard on the rocks at the bottom. When he came up again, his head was cut, and he howled with pain and anger. He was so angry at not catching anything, that he sat down upon the bank of the pool and made ugly faces.

He looked so funny that Jot smiled and showed his white teeth. The ghost saw Jot's smile on the top of the water and became very angry.

"Just you wait, you down there with the laughing teeth!" he screamed. "I'll catch you—like this! I'll tear you apart—like that! And I'll eat you up in the wink of an eye!"

He plunged into the pool and struck his head harder than ever upon the rocks below.

"Stupid, stupid!" called out Jot.

Ligan came up again. He sat down and made worse faces. Jot laughed so hard that he almost fell out of the tree.

Ligan heard him and looked up. He saw the boy and yelled, "Just you wait, you up there, you human child! You are probably a wicked demon. Well, so am I! And I'll tear you limb from limb and eat you up just the same!"

Ligan hopped up and down, biting his fingers in anger. Then he began to bite the trunk of the tree, all around and around. I'll get this tree down, just you wait and see," he shouted.

But Jot cried, "Don't bother to chew down the tree. That will take too long. Look, here's my rope. I'll drop it to you and pull you up. I'll wind the rope around the branch. Let's fight up here in the tree!"

He dropped down one end of the rope. Ligan began to wrap it around his arm, screaming, "Just you wait! Just you wait!"

Jot called to him, "Don't fasten it around your arm, sillyhead. Do it a better way."

"What way?" yelled the ghost.

"Put it around your neck, stupid one—tight, tight, so it can't slip open."

Ligan did exactly as Jot told him. Jot moved to another branch that was over the ground below. He pulled Ligan up slowly into the air, and then, he let the rope go. The ghost crashed down to the hard earth.

"Why do you drop me? Pull me up, you fool, pull me up!" howled Ligan.

Jot pulled him up again, still higher, close to the branch. Again, he let the rope go, and the ghost fell down, harder than ever, upon the rocks below. Jot did that again and again, until every bone in the demon's body was broken, and he was dead.

"You ate our fish, and you wanted to eat us too," said Jot. "You ought to be dead!"

Then Jot clambered down and went into the ghost's large thatched house. He saw a great pile of cooked fish. He ate until he could hold no more. Ligan's *uf*, or cape, was hanging over a roof pole. The *uf* was made of two long, wide strips of matting that were sewn together. One strip was in front, the other was in back. Holes were left for the head and arms. It was large enough to cover Jot completely.

Jot took it down. "Just the thing I need," he said.

First, he used it as a sack. He put in it a great many things that he found in the house. He carried them home and hid them under the house. Then he covered himself with the *uf*, so that he looked like the ghost.

"Now for some fun," he said to himself.

As the sun began to set, he went down to the shore, paddled out to the rocks on the reef, and sat down where Ligan had been before. When his brother, Hak, the king, came by in his canoe,

Jot called out in a deep, hoarse voice, "Hak!" "What!" "Have you fish?" "Yes, ten!" "Well, hand them over, or I'll kill you!"

Hak saw the ghost's cape and gave up his ten fish. When Diu came, there was the same kind of talk, and Diu gave up his nine fish. And so it went with the other brothers—eight, seven, six, five, four, three, and two fine bonitos were handed over to Jot.

When the brothers got back to their large house in Lukaf, they couldn't find their youngest brother. "Where's our Jot, who stayed away from fishing today?" asked Hak. "I don't know," said Diu. "That evil ghost must have eaten the poor boy," said Wal. They looked everywhere, but there was no Jot.

As night came on, they lay down to sleep, hungry and sad. At dawn, they got up, still hungry, and went fishing again. They hoped to catch bonitos and slip by the ghost. They caught the same number of fish as before. Again Jot, dressed like the ghost, was at the reef passage, asking for their catch. And each brother,

sad and unhappy and very hungry, gave him his fish—ten, nine, eight, seven, six, five, four, and three.

Last of all came Riu, the next-to-youngest brother, who was almost as young as Jot. He paddled to the passage in his small canoe, feeling very proud of his two large fish. He and Jot had always played together. They thought a great deal of each other.

"Riu! Have you fish?" called out Jot in a terrible voice. And Riu replied, "Yes, I have two. Please let me keep them."

"Give them to me at once, or I'll eat you!" cried Jot.

Riu held out the two fish. Jot reached out from under the ghost's cape to take them. But just then, Riu saw the tattoo on Jot's arm. He knew his brother at once and quickly took back his two fish.

"Why don't you hand over those fish!" shouted Jot. "I'm really going to eat you, Riu."

"Come and eat me, whenever you're ready," said Riu, and he laughed.

Then Jot laughed too. He looked out from under the *uf* and said, "Riu, I killed Ligan at Aredau. All those fish are there, fresh and good, and breadfruit and coconuts. I've cooked the fish I got from you yesterday. Come and eat with me."

The two lads paddled their canoes to Ligan's house. They ate and ate, until their stomachs were full of good food. Then they lay down upon some mats in the ghost's house and slept.

Next morning, the other brothers got up at dawn. "We'll try fishing for bonito just once more," said Hak. They couldn't find Riu, but they saw a canoe far down on the shore. "It's Riu's!" cried Hak. The brothers went down to see why it was there.

"The ghost must have caught Riu too," said Hak.

The brothers walked to Aredau. They stopped when they saw the ghost's house. Then Hak, the king brother, called the youngest remaining brother, Jol, and whispered, "You're the smallest. Go quietly to that house over there and see what's inside."

Jol crept quietly to the house. He opened the door carefully and peeped inside. He saw no ghosts, but only the two young boys, with full round stomachs, sleeping soundly on the floor. He went inside and shook Jot hard.

"What have you been doing?" he asked.

"Oh, nothing much," replied Jot. "I've killed Ligan. Look at all this food, piles and piles of it. I've been helping myself. Where are the others?"

"Out there."

"Go and call them here."

So Jol went and called his brothers, and they came running. When they saw all the food in the house, they wanted a feast at once, for they had been hungry for many days. But Jot stopped them.

"If you want this food, ask me first," he said. "When I let you, then you may eat, and not before. All this belongs to me."

The brothers sat down and listened while Jot told how he had killed the ghost. They heard about all the things he had taken home. They were proud of their young brother. Finally Hak, the eldest, said, "Up to now, I have been king of Puluwat. Yet I couldn't do anything to get us out of this trouble. In another day or two, we would have had to leave the island and go somewhere else, begging for food. But now that Jot has killed Ligan and has gotten so many things for us, Jot must be king." The brothers agreed.

And that is how young Jot became king of Puluwat.

The Orphan Boys and the Ghost-Woman

A certain chief of Pulusuk Island was worried. There was a terrible famine, and he couldn't understand why.

"Pulusuk always has had more food and fruit than other places," he said. "Our beautiful island is known far and wide for its fine foods. Now we have next to nothing to eat. Even the big fish in the sea are missing. What are we going to do?"

The chief was a kind man. He liked to help the people. His name was Haufelaihok, and he had five daughters and five sons.

In South Pacific islands, sisters and brothers were usually brought up to help each other. And so it was with these ten children. However, they were kind to each other, but to no one else. They didn't like to share what they had with others.

Pulusuk Island still looked beautiful. Tall breadfruit and coconut trees were there, but when the fruit became ripe, it disappeared. No one knew where it went. At last, only a few of the chief's trees had food that could be gathered. The lagoon was full of fish, but the larger ones disappeared. Only the smallest were left.

Days and weeks went by. The people became sick, and many died from starving. Others became weak, crawled into their houses, and lay there dying. No work was done in forest or field or at sea.

Finally, Chief Haufelaihok went from house to house with some of his men. "Look carefully," he said. "Bring to the community house all the people that are starving. I want them near me, so that I can help them."

"How can we feed them all?" asked the men.

"We will all share what food there is," replied the chief.

The community house was a large, long building, strongly built of posts and logs. It had a high roof of coconut-leaf thatch. Inside, rooms were divided off by posts and matting for the chief's family and other important persons. A large space in the center was used as a meeting place.

About a hundred persons were brought to the community house. There they lived, together with the chief and his family. Food was given to all. Sometimes it was nothing but small fish and crabs and a few poor breadfruit, coconuts, and dried-up pandanus.

Chief Haufelaihok went over the island every day, looking for other persons who might be starving. One day, he entered a lonely little leaf-house and found two young boys. They could hardly walk because of hunger. Everyone else in their family had died. Chief Haufelaihok pitied them. He took them to his own house and treated them as his own children.

"These two little boys are your brothers now," he said to his ten children, but they were not pleased.

The chief fed the two young lads special food. Whenever he made sweet palm-juice drink, he gave each boy a large portion, to make them strong. Hunger made the good chief kinder, but it made selfish persons all the more selfish. The ten children were jealous. They waited for a good chance to punish the two boys.

Chief Haufelaihok spent many hours in making the palm-juice drink. If he let coconuts grow from the buds, most of them would disappear before his men could gather them. No one knew who took them. He made the juice in this way: He climbed a coconut palm and tied the long juicy stem that held the bud of the tree. He wrapped it in fiber. Then he cut a slash at the end near the bud. He hung a container under the sweep sap that dripped out. Chief Haufelaihok himself boiled the sap to make the palm-juice drink.

One day, when he was busy with that work, his sons and daughters scolded the two boys and beat them with sticks. "Why should you two have the best of everything?" they shouted.

The two little boys ran away, screaming. The chief heard them and went back to the community house. He saw the two boys hiding behind the building. "Why are you here?" he asked.

The boys answered nothing, for they were afraid of the chief's sons and daughters. The chief brought two bowls of the sweet coconut juice and handed it to them. "Drink it," he said.

The boys drank only one portion, and then they ran away into the forest. The chief looked for them a long time, calling and calling, but the boys ran away all the farther.

It began to rain hard, and they hid under some thick bushes.

Suddenly they saw a gleaming light that seemed to come up out of the ground near a large pond.

One of the orphan boys was braver than the other. "Look, there's a fire. Someone's cooking," he said.

"Oh, no," whispered the timid boy. "That isn't a fire. It's a ghost!"

"Nonsense!" said the brave boy. "That's just a fire."

"Oh, no, no, no, it's a ghost. If we move, it will eat us," said the timid one, beginning to cry.

"We'll just go over there and see," said the brave boy. He took his brother by the hand and pulled him closer to the fire. They saw that it was in front of the stone door of a cave. A woman sat there under a shelter. She was cooking food. It smelled very good to the hungry boys.

"Who are you?" called the brave boy.

"Who, me?" asked the woman.

"Yes, you. Are you a ghost or a human being?"

"I'm human, of course," she answered, "and my name is Afa-issou."

She was lying to the boys, for she was a wicked ghost. It was she who kept taking the food of Pulusuk Island. She had taken the largest fish into the pond near her cave. She hid the food in her cave, piles and piles of it. She ate enough for ten people.

"Come and eat," she said. "I have plenty of food here."

The boys were weak from hunger, but at first, they did not go. "We don't know you," said the brave boy.

"Oh, come along anyhow," said Afa-issou. "See, I'll open the door and show you the food."

She lifted a large stone, and the boys went inside the cave. There, in an oven, were piles of baked taro. The hungry boys reached out their hands, but Afa-issou changed her mind.

"Don't touch them! They're only hot stones!" she cried.

The timid boy drew back, but the brave boy leaned down and picked up a baked taro. "You can't fool me," he said, and he began to eat it.

Afa-issou snatched it away. "If you two want to eat, you must work first," she said. "I have all the large fish of Pulusuk in the pond. Take a fishline and catch me a bonito."

The brave boy sat at the waterhole and caught many fish. His brother also caught some. Afa-issou baked them, and they had a good feast. The ghost-woman did them no harm, since they could catch fish for her. It was the one thing which was hard for her to do.

That went on, day after day. The boys caught fish, and Afa-issou gave them so much food that they became well and strong again.

One day, as the brave boy fished, he thought of good Chief Haufelaihok. "I wonder if he has any food left?" he said to his brother. "We ought to take some to him."

"But his children might harm us," said his brother.

"We'll not let anyone see us," said the brave boy.

The ghost-woman heard them talking, as she sat before the fire, stuffing food into her mouth.

"What are you two saying?" she asked.

"Oh, we're just talking to this bonito that I have on my hook. We want to take him to Chief Haufelaihok, our foster-father."

"What? The great Chief Haufelaihok is your foster-father?" said Afa-issou.

"Yes."

"H'm! Well, well, that's news indeed," she said. "How is he getting along? Has he plenty of food?"

"Hardly any," replied the brave boy. "The chief and his people are starving."

"Well, you may take food to the chief," said Afa-issou. She didn't want the chief to die of hunger. She was afraid of the power he had.

Afa-issou cooked a great deal of taro, breadfruit, coconut, and fish and wrapped it up in parcels. She put them into some large baskets. The boys hung them over poles and carried them.

"Tell the chief that the food is only for himself and his family," said Afa-issou. The boys said nothing.

They were afraid to go to the village by day, and so they took the food at midnight to the large community house. They laid the food at the door. Inside slept all the people, slowly starving to death.

The brave boy crept into the house where Chief Haufelaihok lay, and pinched him until he woke up.

"Who's there?" said the chief, in the darkness.

"I," said the boy, in a low voice.

"Who?"

"I! Get up, get up."

The boy went outside again. The chief followed him, to see who it was that came in the night. "Don't you know us?" asked the boy.

The chief looked and saw two handsome, well-fed lads. "No, I don't," he said.

"Once you kept us here as your sons," said the boy.

"Oh, oh," said the chief. "I know you now! So you're not dead, then?"

"Not at all," said the boy. "We're well and strong and bringing you food."

Chief Haufelaihok was happy. He took the food inside for the night. The boys hid in the brush near the community house and slept there until morning. The chief could not sleep again. At dawn, he blew a *saui*, or conch shell. All the sleepers sprang up quickly.

"Why do you blow the *saui*, Chief Haufelaihok?" they called. "There's nobody to call. We're all here in the house."

"Get up and wash yourselves quickly," said the chief.

The people did so, but they could hardly walk, they were so weak. When they came back from the bathing place, the chief gave each one a baked taro, a baked breadfruit, and a portion of fish. The people were happy. The chief kept on giving food until it was all gone.

The two boys watched from their hiding place. Then they went back to the ghost-woman in the cave.

"The chief needs much more food," they said.

Afa-issou cooked again, many kinds of food. The boys brought it to Chief Haufelaihok at midnight, as before, and then went away again.

Next morning, when the chief blew the *saui* and called the sleeping people, they sprang up happily. "Oh, our chief has food again!" they said. They ate until the food was gone.

The third time the boys came with food, they didn't go away. They stayed in the community house until the sun came up.

When the chief's conch shell awoke the people, there were the two runaway boys, sitting on the floor.

"What! Are you two back again?" said the people.

"Yes."

"Was it you who brought the food for us?"

"Yes."

The people thanked them. Even the ten children of the chief were glad.

"Where did you get the food?" asked Chief Haufelaihok.

The boys said, "Out in the bush lives a strange woman who has a cave under the earth. She has piles of food. She is the one who has taken the food of Pulusuk."

All the people who were able to go ran to the place where the woman lived. When they got there, they could see no one.

The ghost-woman had seen them coming. She had used her magic power to get sand spread over the cave and long grass to grow there.

"The place is right here," said the boys. The people dug with their hands, with sticks, and with stones. They tried to find the opening to the cave, but they did not succeed. They even took large stones and struck the earth, but it did not open.

"You boys are fooling us," they said at last, and they went back again to the community house. The two boys stayed behind.

The brave boy had watched the ghost-woman when she made magic. He remembered it, and he made magic as she had done. He opened the door of the cave. The ghost-woman was gone, but the food was still there.

The boys called the people to come and get the food, and there was a great feast. The ghost-woman never came back. She knew that the people would kill her, if they caught her.

From that time, Pulusuk had plenty of food again.

The Stolen Wife and the Flying Canoe

Long ago, many people believed that ghosts, or spirits, were often near them. These beings had a home in a heaven, but they liked to live on earth as human beings. People sometimes thought

70

that some of the important men and women in their villages were half-ghost and half-human. Legends were told about them.

The ghost-man Jol was such a person. His real home was in Bailol, which was a heaven at the bottom of the sea. It had houses, lands, fruits and flowers, but the deep ocean lay above it.

Jol wandered on earth for a while. Then he stayed in Puluwat Island, in the Eastern Caroline Islands, and became a chief. He married a good woman named Jat. He did not tell anyone that he was a ghost. Jat liked her husband. He was clever and good and kind, but he was a stranger in Puluwat, and her family was angry when she married him.

Five of Jat's relatives used to fish together, and they shared their catch with other members of the family. Even though they didn't like Jol, they wanted him to go fishing with them. But Jol didn't care to spear fish.

"I have to make palm-juice drink today," he said, one day.

The five men went fishing together, but they caught few fish that day. In the evening, they took their share of the palm-juice drink that Jol had made, but they didn't give anything in return.

So it went for days. Whether they caught many or few fish, they gave Jol and Jat little or nothing of their catch. Finally, they said to Jat, "Your husband is too lazy to help us. From now on, you two can go without fish."

Jol loved his beautiful wife very much, but he had no love for her relatives. That day, when he sat down to eat, he said, "What? No fish today?"

"No," replied Jat. "No fish."

"Why not?"

"The men aren't going to give us fish."

Jol was angry. "Well, then," he said, "I'll make a fish trap I know how to do that, and they don't."

The next day, he made a large fish trap. Also, he made some fishhooks out of tortoise shell and tied them to his hair. They stood up all over his head and hung over his shoulders.

"Are you going to catch fish with your hair?" asked Jat, and her husband said. "Just wait and see. Come, go fishing with me."

He took up the fish trap, and they paddled out to the reef. Jat sat in the canoe, while Jol dived and fastened the fish trap to the

71

coral rocks at the bottom. He remained under water for a long time.

Many fish were caught in the trap, and many were caught on the fishhooks in Jol's long hair. When he came to the top again, he called, "Jat! Help me get these fish from my hair."

He was a strange sight to see, with many fish in his hair. They put the fish into their canoe. Then Jol raised up the trap and his wife helped him get it into the canoe. There were many fish. When they got home, they cleaned the fish. They baked them in green leaves in an oven of hot stones. They had a delicious feast. After that, they ate fish every day for a whole month.

When Jat's relatives heard about Jol's great luck at fishing, the men came and asked for some of the fish "You're going to share, aren't you?" they asked.

Jol said, "No, I am not. And you know why."

Then the wives of the five men came and begged for fish, but Jol was hard. "Fish for yourselves," he said.

In about a month, the fish were all eaten. As the moon became small in the west, Jol went fishing again, taking his wife along as before. He handed her a coconut, and said, "Jat, listen to me. I'm going to dive and fasten the fish trap. And this time, I'll be down a long time. Eat this coconut, if you become hungry, but don't spit any of it into the water."

Jol dived down into the water with the fish trap. Jat took the coconut and sat in the canoe. She liked the cool breeze of the trade wind and the sight of the ocean, the lovely green shore of Puluwat Island, and the clouds in the blue sky above her. She was happy. She loved her husband and her home. Through the clear water, she could see Jol, among the coral rocks, far below.

But she forgot what Jol had said. She spit some of the oily coconut crumbs into the sea.

The oil of the coconut drifted off on a fast ocean tide. It went to another place far away to the west. There, a greedy, selfish ghost-man named Haujap, saw the oil. He followed it back to Puluwat reef in his swift sailing canoe. He saw the beautiful wife of Jol sitting alone in the boat.

"Ah, what a prize!" he said. "I must have her."

"I don't want to go," she said. "I want to stay with Jol."

But Haujap took her and carried her to Yap.

When Jol rose to the top again, with the fish in his hair and in the fish trap, he called to his wife, "Jat, help me. Take hold of the trap."

No one answered. He called again. Then he saw that no one was there. He looked all over the reef. His wife had disappeared. He was so sad that he threw away his fish trap and all the fish and paddled back to land.

When he got to shore, everyone asked him, "Where's your wife? Where's Jat?" He replied, "I don't know. But I must get her back again."

He went home and tried to think where she had gone. "If I could only fly like a bird, I might find her," he thought.

Jol finally had an idea. He felled a large, thick breadfruit tree and carved the wood into a flying canoe. It was in the form of an *asaf*, or frigate bird, with body and head, beak and eyes, wings and feet. The frigate bird is a large bird, fierce-looking, with a wide spread of wings. It can stay up in the air a long time without coming down.

When Jol had finished the flying canoe, he crept inside it. He flew high above the clouds and far away, looking for Jat.

He flew, first of all, to the islands east of Puluwat, and then to the south, but he didn't find her. Then he flew to the islands that lay westward. He arrived over Yap. He saw his wife, while he was still in the air in the great flying bird.

The ghost-man, Haujap, had brought Jat to Yap. She thought that she would never get back to Puluwat Island again. She was very sad. She often scolded Haujap. She said to him every day, "If I have to stay here, I must have fish to eat. Get me some."

"I would like to please you, but I haven't any fish," replied Haujap.

"Then go and get some!" she scolded. "Go fishing!"

"But I don't know how to fish," he said.

She gave him no rest. She begged him again and again to get her some fish. Finally, Haujap took up a large fishhook and went to sea in his canoe. He wanted to catch *angarab*, the best fish of all to eat.

That day, Jol came through the air in the flying canoe. Jat was near the house, alone. The wooden bird landed beside her. Jol looked out from it, and she ran to him in joy.

"Come Jat, be quick," he said. He helped her into the flying canoe, and away they flew over the reef. Then they went around slowly over Haujap's canoe.

When he saw the frigate bird, he thought it was alive. "Oh, what a prize!" he said. "I must have that *ahaf*. I must catch it alive."

But how was he to catch such a large *ahaf?* How could he make it come down to him?

"I'll catch it with fish for bait," he said. He had caught a hundred fine *angarab* that day. He threw them into the air, one after the other. He hoped that the bird would fly down to the rocks to eat them. But the frigate bird came down and caught each fish in mid-air. It was Jol who reached out his hand and took them. Haujap did not know that the bird was a wooden flying canoe, and that Jat and Jol were inside.

Jat laughed and said, "Take every fish, Jol. Let Haujap pay for the trouble he has given us."

Jol said, "We have all his fish now. Lean out, Jat. Let him see you. Tell him you're going to fly back to Puluwat."

Jat leaned out and called, "Haujap! Haujap! I'm leaving you. I'm flying back to Puluwat!"

Haujap looked up. He saw Jat and was angry. He hopped up and down, yelling loudly. Finally, he fell down dead, and that was the end of him.

Jol flew away to Puluwat Island with Jat. He said on the way, "My dear wife, when we get to Puluwat Island, your home, there you must stay. As for me, I must soon leave you. I must go back to my home in Bailol, at the bottom of the ocean."

Jat looked at him in surprise. "Don't you really know what I am?" said Jol. "I'm a ghost, and I must go."

So Jat went back to her home in Puluwat and stayed there. Soon after, Jol dived into the sea. He turned himself into a *neinjol* and swam back to his heaven. The *neinjol* is a pretty fish, red in color, and about as long as a man's hand. It has a ghostly kind of face, like Jol's.

Stories About Parents and Children

Mothers and fathers in Micronesia usually let the children have much free time. Most girls and boys under ten years of age did little work. They took care of younger sisters and brothers, and sometimes they helped to carry things, but they had many hours of play.

Brothers and sisters were taught to have respect for each other, and there were legends about brothers and sisters who helped each other. There also were legends about brothers in a large family who were jealous of each other. The youngest one sometimes was the favorite son of the mother or father. Often, he was more industrious, obedient, and clever than his. elder brothers.

Magic had an important part in the stories. Number four was a lucky number. In stories, a hero would try three times to do a deed, and he would fail, each time. When he tried the fourth time, he had luck.

Sometimes, a father was the hero of a story about a family, and sometimes, it was the mother. There were many legends about mothers and their children. There were legends about a boy or girl who loved their mother, or a mother who did wonderful things for her child.

Here are some legends about parents and children.

The First Breadfruit Tree

Sometimes, an island in the Pacific Ocean disappeared and was never seen again. Perhaps an earthquake broke it up. Perhaps high waves made by a typhoon washed away its top. The old people sometimes told stories about islands that used to be in certain places long ago, but were there no longer.

There was once a small island called Ngibtal. It lay outside the reef near Ngiwal village, on Babelthuap Island, in the Palau Islands. On that little island, there stood a strange, large tree. People came from everywhere to see it. Whenever anyone cut off one of its branches, out came live fishes, large enough for food.

The people on Ngibtal Island didn't have to go to the lagoon or outside the reef for fish. All they had to do was to cut off a branch from the tree and catch the fish in baskets. In that way, they got all the fish they could use. They were very happy about their good luck.

Every time a branch was cut, there was heard the sad crying of a woman, somewhere on the island. She could be heard, begging the people not to cut off the branches of the tree.

"Who is this woman that cries when we cut the tree?" the people asked. "Let's ask her why she does this."

They went around the island looking for her. At last, they found her. She was a wise woman who lived by herself. They asked why she cried when they cut a branch of the tree.

"Because it's a tree that will grow bread for you," she said. "It's the only one in the world. If you keep on cutting it, branch by branch, then, one day, it will die."

At that time, no one had ever eaten breadfruit or known a breadfruit tree. "A tree growing bread?" cried the people. "Can there be such a thing?"

"You already have that tree," she said. "You should keep it always."

"What shall we do now?" asked the people.

"First of all," replied the wise woman, "stop cutting the tree. Then, after a while, it will have large green fruit. It will be good food for you. Just wait and see."

The people stopped cutting the tree. They went again to the lagoon to catch fish. Soon, the tree gave them breadfruit, and the people learned how to cook it and eat it. Since that time, breadfruit has been one of their best foods.

The little island of Ngibtal, on which grew the first bread-fruit tree, can no longer be seen. It sank into the sea, a long time later. Some people say that it was covered by great tidal waves. Some Palauan legends tell other stories about it. Today, only part of Ngibtal Island can be seen in shallow water, beyond the main reef of Babelthuap Island. Ships cannot pass over it, for the water is not deep enough. Sometimes fishermen paddle their outrigger canoes over it.

"There's Ngibtal, the home of the first breadfruit tree," they say, looking down through the clear water.

Artists. in the Palau Islands used to paint pictures about this story upon the walls of the men's clubhouses. They painted the large tree, with the fish jumping from the trunk. They painted the cut-off branches. They painted the men with axes and spears. Sometimes in the pictures, there was also the wise woman of Ngibtal, who had been like a mother to all the people.

The Woman of Ngerehokl

In the village of Ngerdamau, in the Palau Islands, there once lived a woman who had neither husband nor son. She had only a little daughter, whom she loved dearly.

The mother and child were very poor. They did not always have food enough, for the child was too young to work. But they had each other, and they were happy together.

When the child was born, the mother already was forty years old. She was beginning to be fat and to have gray hair and wrinkles. That worried her. She wanted to look fresh and beautiful again.

"My daughter should have a young, pretty mother," she thought.

One day, she heard about a strange, wonderful river in the mountains. It was between her village and the next one. The

79

river was called Ngerehokl. People said that old people dived into it and became young again.

The mother could hardly wait to go there. She started out with the child the next day, walking the long way to the mountains.

"Where are we going?" asked the child.

"To see a river," replied the mother. She told the child nothing more, but she thought about the surprise the child would have.

They walked a long way through a dark forest. They came at last to the river Ngerehokl, in a valley in the mountains. It was a beautiful place, with many flowers and singing birds. There, the river made a deep pool among trees and rocks.

The mother said to her daughter, "I'm going away for a while, my child, but I won't go far. Just stand here on the rocks and wait for me."

She left the child and went to the pool. She dived into the deep water. The child stood a little distance away on the shore and waited.

The mother came to the top of the water again and swam to shore. She was no longer old, fat, wrinkled, and gray. She was beautiful and young. She ran to her child. "My little daughter, how do you like me?" she asked.

The little girl looked at her but did not smile.

"Don't you know me?" said the mother. "See how beautiful I am!" The child shook her head.

"Come, dear child," said the mother, "let s go home now." But the child would not leave the place where she was standing.

"I'm waiting for my mother," she said.

Again and again, the woman told the child that she was indeed her mother. Again and again, the child shook her head and would not go home with her.

When the mother tried to take her, the little one became angry. "You're not my mother!" she cried. She ran around on the rocks, stamping her feet and jumping up and down. "You're much younger than my mother. I want my mother!" At last, she threw herself down and cried.

The mother ran back to the river. She dived into it several times, until her old face and form came back to her. Then she called to her child, "Here I am!"

The little girl ran to her mother's arms. "I've been waiting for you a long time," she said. The mother had learned a strange lesson.

It was a rule of the river that no one should dive in it but once. The woman broke the rule by diving several times. From that time, it has been just a common river, like all other rivers. No one can become young again by diving into it today. But since the name of the river is Ngerehokl, people always remember the woman as the "woman of Ngerehokl."

The footprints of the little girl can still be seen, where she jumped up and down on the rocks beside the river.

Debolār, The First Coconut

Most things of great value in the world have come from ordinary beginnings, and so it was with the coconut tree.

An old Marshallese legend tells that long ago, no one had ever seen a tree. There never yet had been any in all the world. When the first one grew, it was thought to be a wonderful thing. It was a coconut tree, and that great blessing was born from a woman. It grew from a living baby.

Some persons don't believe this, but isn't there on the top end of each coconut a little face with nose, mouth, and two eyes?

Likileo is a place on the ocean side of Woja Island, in beautiful Ailinglaplap Atoll. In Likileo, there once lived a good woman named Limōkare, who had several children. She had no idea that one of them would become famous.

Her first child, a son named Lōkam, looked much like other boys. But when her second child was born, all the people of the village came to see, for it was a very strange baby indeed. It was a coconut. Small and green, and with a clever little face that had eyes, nose, and mouth, but still—a coconut!

The mother was pleased with her baby. She named him Debolār. No one had ever seen a coconut before, and the people of the village admired the odd little baby. All, that is, except his elder brother, Lōkam, who didn't like him at all.

"Why do you keep that queer-looking thing?" he said to his mother, again and again. "Kill it, and throw it away."

"No!" cried his mother. "Debolār is my baby, I love him."

She gave him her milk, and he drank until his little belly grew full and round. If there is a person who doesn't believe that Debolār could drink milk, let him look inside a coconut. It is filled with milk, even as Debolār was, that day long ago. The milk is rich and sweet and is good food. Like Debolār, many babies in the Pacific islands today have no other food but coconut milk. It makes them fat and happy.

The mother gave Debolār the best of care. She wove him a little basket. She used *koba*, or bamboo, which was of great value in those days. It didn't grow in Woja Island but sometimes came drifting in on the tide. Limōkare put the baby in the basket and hung it up. She rocked him and sang him to sleep.

Lōkam, the elder brother, thought that was very silly. "I won't be a brother to such a thing," he said. "I don't care to be in the same house with it."

After a while, Lōkam went away and found another home. All the same, he came once in a while, just to look at the baby.

Debolār grew larger and larger. Soon, he learned to talk and to understand what people said. In that way, he found out that Lōkam was asking their mother to get rid of her baby.

"Don't listen to that brother of mine," said Debolār to his mother. "He'll never be of much use to you. I'm small, and I look odd, it's true. But I'll be valuable some day. I'll make you comfortable and happy. Just wait and see."

"Don't worry, my son," said Limōkare, "I'm not going to throw you away. You came into this world for a good reason."

"And so I did," replied Debolār. "I came into this world to be eaten and worn and used."

"Eaten, my poor child!" exclaimed his mother. "And worn! And used!"

"Yes, Mother," said Debolār. "That's what I'm here for."

One day, he said to his mother, "The time has come for you to bury me under your window."

The window was made of thatch. It swung out, a little way from the ground, making a shelter.

His mother was surprised. "Bury you alive, my poor little baby?" she cried.

"Yes, alive," replied Debolār. "I'm not going to die. I will live. I'll come back to you and stay with you always."

"How can you come back, and how shall I know you, my child?" asked Limōkare.

"I'll be a tree," said Debolār.

"And what's that, my son?"

"Wait and see," he said. "I'll be very small at first, and I'll need your care. But I'll grow, and I'll have many parts. Every one of them will be useful. And I'll have dozens of children and hundreds of grandchildren."

He and his mother had a long talk. He told what the parts of his body would be, and how they could be used. It was a strange story, but his mother believed it.

The mother buried the coconut baby under her window, as he had told her to do. She looked there many times a day.

The people of the village didn't believe that she would see Debolār again. "He's gone forever," they said.

"And so much the better," said the elder son, Lōkam. "You did right to put him into the ground. Just let him stay there."

One day, the mother saw a small, green sprout. "Debolār is coming," she said. It was a leaf, folded around itself. She opened it carefully.

"How beautiful!" she said. "It looks like the wing of the flying fish."

84

She gave the little coconut sprout a name, *drirjojo*. The word *drir* meant "sprout" and *jojo* meant "flying fish." As the leaf grew and spread open, and other leaves came, she gave the tree new names. The coconut tree has them to this day.

People came from far and near to see the first tree in all the world. They called it *ni*, which became the Marshallese word for "coconut."

The little tree became tall and beautiful and strong. It grew away from the window, high in the air. At its top grew waving leaves that made cool shade for Limōkare. She often sat beneath them and wove mats from them.

Limōkare told the people the things that Debolār had told her. She told them how the parts of the tree could be used—the leaves, the wood, the bark, the roots, the nuts, the husks, and the juices. The tree was a great blessing to her. It gave her many useful things.

The elder brother, Lōkam, no longer wanted Debolār to be killed. He also liked the gifts of the coconut tree. He boasted about his brother.

"We kept him, and we cared for him, and we planted him," he said. "Now the rest of you may have his coconut children and grandchildren. They will be your food, your drink, your oil, your clothes, your wood, and your houses."

He would look around, then, to see if all the people were listening. Then he would say, "Don't forget. I'm his brother."

Debolār's Brother, Lōkām

Stories about the first coconut were told in many places in the Marshall Islands. They were not always told in the same way. Here is another story of Debolār and his family.

At one time, they lived in Enibiñ, a part of Ailinglaplap Island. Limōkare was a wise, good woman, the sister of the famous king, Irilik. They were of the royal clan, or Iroij, and were known to people in many islands.

Limōkare had, first of all, a son named Lōkam. Then she had a strange baby that was a coconut. He grew to be a tree, the first one in the world. She called him Debolār. Later, she had two other sons. They were small boys when Debolār had grown to a tree.

The elder brother, Lōkam, was jealous of Debolār. He moved away to a place of his own, but he used to come to his mother's home often. When the first young green leaves and nuts came on the coconut palm, Lōkam couldn't wait. He gathered a few and put a few pieces into his mouth.

"They're bitter!" he cried. He spit them out and threw away the leaves and nuts. "Let's chop down that thing called a tree," he said to his mother. "It's no good."

"No," she said. "I'm going to keep it and tend it always."

There were dozens of young coconuts on the tree. She made them all *tabu* for Lōkam until they were ripe. "You just leave them alone," she said.

Many nuts ripened. They fell to the ground, and young coconut-palm sprouts began to grow. Soon, Limōkare had a great many young coconut trees. Even Lōkam became proud of his brother. He said to his mother, "I'd like to take some coconuts over to my proud uncle, the Iroij Irilik. I want to show him how wonderful our Debolār is. Irilik hasn't anything like that."

"Take him some, then," said Limōkare, "Let your two little brothers go along with you."

Limōkare and her brother, the great Iroij, were good friends. She wanted her children to respect their uncle.

Lōkam gathered a great pile of ripe nuts. He husked them and put them into large baskets. He threw the husks into the sea. They drifted far away to the westward, where the Iroij Irilik lived. The great chief picked up the strange-looking things and looked at them. "They have strong fibers, which would make good twine and rope," he said.

He soaked the husks in sea water, keeping them in place with stones. Then he was able to pull out the fibers. He made several kinds of twine and rope by rolling the fibers upon his thigh. All the people came to see them.

Then, Lōkam came in his outrigger canoe, bringing his two little brothers and the coconuts from the tree, Debolār. His uncle thanked him and asked, "Where did you get these wonderful things?"

"My mother got them from a strange thing called a tree," replied Lōkam.

Lōkam saw the twine that his uncle was making. He wanted to learn how to do it. So Irilik sat down and showed him.

While the two men were busy, rolling the fibers, Lōkam's little brothers ran around and played. They made a great deal of noise. They played the game called *anirep*. They found a ball that some larger boys had left on the ground. It was a square-cornered ball, made of soft pandanus fibers, tightly folded and tied.

In playing *anirep*, the game is to kick the ball sidewise, front-wards, or backwards. The players must keep it in the air, all the time. It is played to different kinds of rhythm—two-rhythm, or three-rhythm, or four-rhythm. The players clap their hands and keep time for the kicking.

With two-rhythm clapping, the playing is slow, one, two—one, two—one, two. Everybody starts the game with that slow rhythm. Then the clapping becomes faster. Soon the players are kicking fast—one-two-three, one-two-three, and then one-two-three-four, one-two-three-four. Those who miss are out of the game. The players shout and laugh when someone drops the ball. Sometimes they throw small pebbles at the losers.

The two little brothers of Lōkam lost the ball many times. They threw pebbles at each other, screaming and laughing. One of the pebbles fell upon the arm of the Iroij Irilik.

Lōkam turned to the boys. "Stop that noise!" he shouted angrily. "Have you no respect for your uncle, the great Iroij?"

"Go ahead and play." said the king to his small nephews. Then he spoke to Lōkam. "Children don't make noise to be bad," he said. "Leave them alone. Let them laugh and play."

When the Iroij had a large roll of twine, he laid it inside his house. The two little boys soon found it. They played with it for a while. Then they sat down outside and began to tie a net with it. The net grew and grew in their small hands, until it was the largest one that ever had been seen. The boys couldn't stop tying the net until all the twine was used up. Irilik and Lōkam came and watched.

"That net shall hold up the sky," said Irilik.

In those days, the sky hung very low. Sometimes, it touched the heads of tall persons and the tops of houses, It was heavy work to push up the sky to gather coconuts from tall trees. And besides, there wasn't enough breeze under the sky. It often was hard to breathe.

After a while, the net was finished and lay in piles around the house. Then the Iroij Irilik made magic and sang a chant.

First, Irilik sang to the boys. He told each one to turn himself into a *keār*, the swift white sea bird that flies high in the sky. Then he sang something like this:

"Oh, *keār*, white, fast sea birds,
Take up the net, take up the net,
Catch the sky and lift it high!"

The people didn't understand what the king sang in the chant, but they saw the boys change into white birds. The two birds took up a corner of the great net in their strong beaks. They flew with it toward the east. There they pushed up the sky and fastened it with the net. Then they flew with the net to the north, to the west, to the south. Last of all, they flew high in the middle, rounding up the sky and making the arch of heaven. They fastened the net so that it would stay forever, far above men's heads. And there it still is.

The people were happy. They felt free, with the sky lifted up. They breathed more easily. They thanked the Iroij, but he said, "It has been done by my sister's three wonderful sons, Ḍebolār and the two little boys."

Lōkam was jealous of his three brothers. He got ready to sail back home to Enibiñ. Before he went, he made fun of the place where his uncle lived.

"Why don't you come over to our part of the island and see how green it is?" he asked. "This land of yours is a poor place. It isn't one-tenth as good as ours."

The Iroij Irilik was angry. He looked at his nephew for a moment. Then he said, "Very well! I'll come and visit you, if my servants may come too."

"Let them come also and see," said Lōkam.

Irilik and his servants sailed away to Enibiñ. Lōkam sailed ahead. He ordered his people to get fruit, fish, and other foods.

"Bring only the best," he said. "Let him see how well I live."

Irilik and his men ate a great deal of food, but much remained. Then Irilik gave magical power to his servants. He said to them. "Spoil the crops and the food of Lōkam."

His men obeyed. One servant made all Lōkam's cooked food smell badly; another filled it with worms; a third man put black spots on the fruits; another made the breadfruit sour; and another turned all the leaves of the trees white and dry.

"I thought you said you had wonderful crops," said Irilik to his nephew. Then he sailed away.

In that way, Lōkam's uncle punished him. But Irilik didn't want Lōkam and his people to starve. He sent two kinds of fish to the shores of Enibiñ, the *melemel* and the *lejabwil* fish. Large schools of those fish are still there. When he thought that Lōkam had been punished long enough, Irilik took away the curse.

The net which the two young boys made still holds up the sky and keeps it from falling down upon the earth. When a heavy dark cloud is above them, all ready to fall, the people do not worry, for the fiber net holds it up. The rain falls through the small holes in the net, which separate it into raindrops.

The Blind Mother

In the Mortlock Islands, Satawan Island has always been a special place for magic. People once believed the stories of strange things done there.

"Did it happen in Satawan?" they asked. "Then it's entirely possible." Here is an old story of magic in Satawan.

There was once a woman who had become old and blind. Her husband had died, but she had a son and a young daughter. One day, she said to the son, "I hope you won't marry while I'm still living. You are the only one left to take care of me and your little sister."

"I'll never leave you, mother," said the young man, "even though I might marry some day."

One day, when he came home from fishing in the lagoon, he saw a young, beautiful girl standing on shore. She called to him in a soft voice, and he went to her. They talked together for a long time. He wanted her as his wife.

He went home and told his mother. At first, she asked him not to marry. He asked again and again.

"Marry her, then," she said, "but bring her home with you. We can all live together here. Explain to her that I am old and blind and that your sister is but a child. Tell her that we need your help in order to live."

The son brought the young wife home. In a short while, she began to scold. "I don't like to live here," she said. "I don't care to cook food for an old blind woman and a child. I am going home to my mother and father."

She wanted the young man to go with her. He liked to please his lovely wife, so he went with her. For a long time, he almost forgot about his home. He never went there. His mother and sister had to get along without help. Sometimes, they had no food.

One night, he waited for the tide until late at night. Then he went torch fishing on the reef. A heavy rain came. He ran for shelter to a small leaf-hut that stood near the shore. There was a light inside. He saw a poor young woman with a sick baby in her arms. She was trying to keep up a fire among the stones and to warm something for it to eat.

She took good care of the child, though it was the middle of the night. The young man watched her. Suddenly, he remembered his own mother.

"She cared for me, when I was little and helpless," he thought. "She's old and blind now. I must help her."

After that, he went to see her and was kind to her again. When he went fishing, he gave her the largest fish. He gave her the finest bananas and the best taro.

His selfish young wife wanted the best for herself. She was jealous of the old mother and the young sister.

After a while, the son became careless again. He let his wife take the food, instead of going to see his mother himself.

One day, the young man caught only two fish, a large one and a small one. "Cook the large one and take it to my mother," he said to his wife. "The small one will do for us."

The wife was angry, but she said nothing. When her husband left the house, she went out and caught four or five small lizards. She knew very well that no one eats lizards, unless he is starving. She cooked them, wrapped them in green leaves, and took them to her husband's old mother, instead of bringing her the fish.

"Your son sent you food," she said.

After she had gone, the old mother began to eat the food. Since she was blind, she could not see what she was eating. She gave some of it to her little daughter, and the child began to cry.

"You're eating lizards!" she said.

The old mother thought about that for a while. Finally, she said, "Never mind. This food was sent to me by my son. I'll eat what he sends. You don't need to eat it. Save the rest for me. I'll have it for my next meal."

The next day, she said to her daughter, "Help me make a feast for your brother. There's very little to cook, but we'll give him the best we have."

The mother told her daughter to go and bring her brother to the house. The child went and called him to the little feast.

"Welcome home," said the blind mother. "We eat special fish, my son." She gave him some of the food.

The young man put his fingers into the coconut bowl and
ate. But as he ate, he saw that his fingers, one by one, were turning into claws, and it frightened him. His mouth slowly became
wide and ugly, but he couldn't stop eating.

"He's turning into a lizard!" cried his little sister.

When the young man finished his meal, he saw that his whole
body had turned into that of a huge, ugly lizard. His mother
and his sister were crying.

"Why did this happen to me?" he cried.

"It must be because you sent us lizards for food," said his
mother.

He knew then, that his wife had brought lizards to his mother.
He knew that she was a selfish young woman, but he still wanted
most of all to please her. So he crawled away, without another
word, and went home to her.

When his young wife saw him coming, she ran away, screaming. He crawled after her, calling to her, "Don't run away!"

She ran and ran. He followed, along the paths in the woods, down the village road, and up and down the hills.

"This is partly your fault," he cried. "You sent lizard food to my mother, and so I've become like this. But I still have the mind and the heart of a man, and I'm your husband. You mus stay with me!"

The young wife ran away from him all the faster. At last she ran into the lagoon and swam away. The big lizard swam after her, across the lagoon. They swam through the passage in the coral reef. They swam far out in the deep blue ocean, until they both were drowned. Neither one was ever seen again.

Ohokasau and His Mother

A long time ago, there was a boy named Ohokasau. He lived with his mother in a little leaf hut on an island of Mokil Atoll. The hut stood on a faraway shore, hidden among trees and brush. Other people seldom came there. The soil was too thin for most food plants to grow well.

Ohokasau and his mother were very poor. He had no other children to play with, and he was lonely.

"Why do we live here, all by ourselves?" he asked one day, when he was about eight years old.

"Because our relative, the king, is a cruel man," said his mother. "Long ago, when your father died, the king wanted us killed. But I ran away with you to this far island. He has never found us. He thinks we died long ago."

"Where is this king?" asked the boy.

"He lives on another island and rules the whole atoll," replied his mother. "He must never find out that we are alive."

"Why did he want us to die?"asked the boy.

"Because you are the rightful king, my child," said his mother.

The boy thought about what his mother had told him. He was a good lad. He helped his mother raise taro and find shore fish and crabs. She was a chief's daughter, and she had learned a great deal when she was young. She taught him everything that she could remember.

Ohokasau grew tall and strong. He loved his mother, but he longed to know other children. Sometimes, boys came with fishermen, and he talked with them.

When he was about thirteen years old, he heard that the boys of the king's village, on the other island, were going to have a race. They were going to make canoes and sail them on a certain day. There would also be games and a feast. Ohokasau wanted to go.

"We belong in the king's village," he said to his mother. "Let me go and take part in the races."

He asked so often that finally, his mother agreed. She knew that he soon must take his place among the men of the atoll.

There was no grown man to help Ohokasau make his racing canoe. He worked hard to make the little boat. He carved it from a piece of log about four feet long, using a knife made of oyster shell.

Boys about twelve to eighteen years of age made their own small canoes and outriggers. They stained them with gay colors. Each had a sail made of leaves and fastened to a slender mast. The canoes were too small to hold a boy, but they could go fast over the water. When Ohokasau's canoe was completed, he colored it in red and black.

"It's a beautiful boat," said his mother. "Be careful. Don't let anyone know who you are."

Early in the morning of the important day, Ohokasau took the little canoe under his arm and went to the meeting place. The other boys greeted him and looked at his boat. Some boats were longer than his, and some were shorter. Some had higher masts, and some had lower ones. The outriggers were not alike, either.

Ohokasau was happy to see all the people. There were men, women, boys, girls, and children of all ages.

The king sat in a place of honor on shore. Around him were his friends and members of his family. The time came when the boys were all in the lagoon, knee-deep in water holding their canoes. The signal was given, and the boys let them go.

The little boats sailed away, over the lagoon. Behind each one, a young boy walked or swam in the shallow water. Ohokasau was the only stranger.

"Who is this boy?" asked the people. "Where does he come from? His canoe is very fast."

On, on went the little boats. They went around a coral rock, far out in the lagoon. Then they turned back to shore, tacking against the wind with the help of their owners. Ohokasau's canoe was ahead of the others, but two larger ones came close. He talked to his canoe. "Sail, sail, my boat," he said. "Let no one pass you!"

His canoe won the first race. There were a number of races. The other boys tried to beat the strange boy's boat, but his canoe was always far ahead. It won all the races.

Then something happened. A young girl with a proud walk went down to the water. She took up Ohokasau's canoe, and went away with it. Ohokasau didn't know that she was the daughter of the king.

"That's my canoe! Put it down!" he cried. The girl went on.

Ohokasau ran after her. "That's my boat! You can't have it!" he cried.

He was very angry. He stopped the girl and took hold of the

canoe. The girl tried to keep it. Then he slapped her on the cheek. She dropped the boat and began to scold and cry. Ohōkasau took up his canoe and walked home. He did not stay for the other games and the feast.

When the day was over, the king saw a red spot on his daughter's cheek. "What happened to your face?" he asked.

"A strange boy struck me," she said.

"What boy?" demanded the king.

"The one whose boat won the races," she replied.

"Who is that boy?" shouted the king.

The girl did not know. So, the next day, he called the people of the village to a meeting. "Who was the boy that won the races?" he asked. No one could tell him.

The king called some soldiers. "Get that boy! Look in every corner of all the islands of the atoll. Don't come back without him. I'll show him if he can slap my daughter and still live."

The soldiers found Ohokasau and brought him to the king. "Did you strike my daughter yesterday?" asked the king.

"Yes," replied Ohokasau, "but not without good reason."

"Never mind the reason!" said the king. "Climb that tall coconut palm at once."

Ohokasau climbed to the top of the coconut palm.

"Now you stay there!" shouted the king. He told his men to gather armfuls of dry coconut leaves and pile them high around the tree. While they did it, a dark cloud came over the sky.

"Set fire to the leaves!" said the king. "Burn up both tree and boy."

The men made fire and the flames went high. Just then, a heavy rain fell from the dark cloud and put out the fire.

"Let the boy live! Let him live!" cried the people. They thought that Ohokasau had been saved by spirits in the sky.

The king had to let Ohokasau go home. "It's the wrong day," he said. "Come back tomorrow."

The next day, Ohokasau came again. "Dig a hole there," said the king. He pointed to a spot where the ground was soft. Ohokasau took a coconut shell and dug. The people felt sorry for him. By and by, the hole in the ground was so deep that he could hardly be seen.

"Now drop that large rock into the hole and crush him," the king said to his soldiers.

The men did so. They didn't know that the boy had dug a tunnel, off to one side, into which he had crept. He had left the coconut shell in the hole. The people heard the shell crack as the rock fell upon it.

"Good! Now he's dead," said the king.

"Poor, poor boy," said the people.

Ohokasau dug the tunnel up to the top of the ground and came out, safe and well. "He's alive, he's alive!" cried the people. "What a brave boy he is!"

"It's the wrong day," said the king. "Come back tomorrow." So Ohokasau went home.

The third morning, he stood before the king again. "Take hold of him!" shouted the king. "Carry him to a fast canoe and take him far out to sea. Throw him overboard, where it's too far to swim back."

The men took Ohokasau and sailed out to sea. But something happened. One story says that high waves made them all sick, except Ohokasau. Another story says that Ohokasau struck each man on the head with a club, and they could not move. Still another story tells that the men liked the boy and didn't want him killed. They pretended to be sick, so that his life might be spared.

Whatever happened, there came Ohokasau back to land again, safe and well, with all the men lying around him in the canoe, as though they were dead.

The king was on the beach, waiting to hear that the boy was drowned. When he saw Ohokasau, he stamped his feet. "You here again?" he yelled. "Why don't you die?"

"Because I am the rightful king," said Ohokasau. "I have had enough of your cruelty. Let there be an end to it now." He took his oyster-shell knife from his belt and killed the wicked man.

Ohokasau brought his mother to the village. She told the people the story of their life, and so Ohokasau became king of Mokil Atoll.

"You're a wonderful young man," the people said. "We know that you will be a famous king."

The Brave Boy and the Serpent

Aimeliik is a wide, beautiful place near the shore in Babelthuap Island, Palau. Nobody remembers when the first people came, but it was long ago. Children like to hear stories of strange things that happened there in the old days.

Once, a huge serpent lived in the island. He used to eat some of the people, when he was hungry. The people tried to kill him, but they were not successful. Year by year, the serpent took some of them. They lived always in fear.

One day, the chief said, "I must take you away from the village. You will have to give up your houses and good lands forever. We will start life in another part of Babelthuap, far from Aimeliik."

That was hard for the people to do, but they agreed to go. Soon, there was great excitement. The people packed up their things and got into outrigger canoes. Would there be canoes enough for all? They were loaded very high. Many parcels had to be thrown out at the last moment. Even the chief had to leave some things behind.

A poor young woman went from canoe to canoe with her simple belongings. She tried to find a place, but no one made room for her. "Find someone else to take you," they all said.

One by one, the canoes sailed away over the lagoon. When the last one went, she was left behind on shore. She stood there crying. Then she went back to the village. She was afraid to stay there, for the serpent knew that place very well. She took the things she needed and walked far up the mountains to a hidden valley. There she built a small hut for herself out of leaves.

In the daytime, she hid herself in the dark hut. At night, she went out and hunted for food. She never made a fire for cooking. If the serpent saw smoke above the trees, he would know that someone was there. She always ate her food raw.

She lived in that way for some time. Then, a baby boy was born to her. She was very happy to have him. He grew fast and was strong and clever. She watched over him day and night and kept him from going near the serpent.

One day, when the boy was ten years old, he asked his mother why they lived without any people around them. She told him the story of the large serpent and showed him the village of Aimeliik, down by the shore. She told him why they could never make a fire.

The boy wanted to obey his mother. But from that time, he thought about killing the serpent. Finally, he had an idea.

He gathered together large bundles of dry firewood. He piled them upon the edge of a cliff, on the mountainside. Day after day, he worked from early morning until night. Then he gathered large rocks and dragged them to the cliff. It was hard work for a young boy. At last, there was a great pile of them beside the wood.

Then he asked his mother to show him how to build a large fire.

His mother was frightened. She cried out, "What a poor son you are! You want to make a fire! I have told you why we must never do such a thing. If the serpent sees the smoke of even one small fire, we won't live much longer, my son."

"I'm quite ready to meet that serpent," said the boy. "Let me have a fire."

Finally, she consented. They rubbed dry sticks together to get sparks and let them catch fire in dry coconut husks. Soon there were flames that burned the wood. The smoke went higher and higher in the sky.

The serpent was hungry. When he saw smoke in the valley, he went there. He was so large and strong, as he moved along, that thick breadfruit trees and tall coconut palms fell crashing down.

The poor mother saw the serpent. She ran around and around her poor little leaf-hut, crying. She felt sure that the serpent would take her boy and then come and get her.

The boy stood beside the pile of stones on the cliff. He held a long pole and tended the fire. The stones became hotter and hotter. "Let the serpent come. I am ready for him!" he said.

The serpent came into the valley and crawled up to the cliff. His eyes shone like fire, and he opened his ugly mouth. Quickly the boy pushed hot stones into it, working fast with his long pole.

The serpent did not want to swallow hot stones, but he swallowed a great many of them before he knew what was happening. Then, it was too late to stop. By that time, he could not close his mouth. Soon he rolled over and died.

The boy's mother came running to him. "My brave son, you have killed the serpent!" she said.

The boy cut open the serpent's belly and took out the bladder. He put it in a wooden dish which once had belonged to the chief of Aimeliik. Then he carried the dish down to the lagoon and put it in the water. Before it floated away, he spoke to it.

"When you reach the place where the chief and his people now live," he said, "they will ask you questions. Remain just as you are, until they ask if you are part of the serpent of Aimeliik. Then swell up very large."

The dish floated away on the tide. In a few days, it came to the place where the people lived, in a new village named Ngebukud. They all came running to see the strange thing. The chief looked at the wooden dish and the bladder. He knew that the dish had once been his own. He asked many questions. Nothing happened. Then he asked, "Are you part of the serpent of Aimeliik?"

The bladder began to swell. It swelled more and more, until it was as large as a basket. The chief knew then that the serpent had been killed.

"Now we can go back home to Aimeliik!" he said.

The people were glad. They ran to pack up their things. They got the canoes ready. In a few days, they sailed back to their old home.

The boy was ready for them. He made some sharp spears and waited at the shore. He was angry with the people, because they had been cruel to his mother.

The canoes crossed the lagoon, but the boy would not let them come near the shore. "You have no right to come here!" he shouted. "Stay back, or there will be a big battle, I can tell you! I will fight all of you."

The chief and his people had nothing to fight with. "Please, let us go back to our land without any trouble," they said.

"Never!" shouted the brave boy, waving his spears. "You have no land in Aimeliik now. Just remember that my mother was left here alone, when the rest of you went away. I intend to make you pay for it."

"We did wrong. We will never do anything like that again," said the people. But the boy raised the spears still higher.

Finally, the chief said, "You are a brave boy. We will give you whatever you ask, if you will let us stay."

The boy thought it over. "Very well, then," he said at last. "I will take half of the land for my mother and myself. The rest of you may share the other half. But don't forget, the poor people of our village must always be helped. That must be a rule in Aimeliik from this time."

The chief and the people agreed. They all settled in Aimeliik again. The brave boy became a rich man and a leader of the people. His mother was happy.

The pile of stones is still on Babelthuap Island. Children go up the mountain behind Aimeliik to look for them. They find them on the cliff, just where the brave boy put them, long ago.

The Fighting Champion and his Young Brother

Some legends were so old that the names of villages and islands in them were forgotten. Even the names of the heroes were lost. Yet the stories lived on, perhaps because of some great thought in them.

Such a story was told in Truk about two brothers. It was a story where truth was victorious over lies. Perhaps that is why the story lived such a long time.

In a certain island, the people were great fighters. They loved to fight. They knew how to make weapons of war and how to use them well.

Those were the days of hand-to-hand fighting. Only the strong and the brave dared to go to war. If enemies came by land, the fighters of that island went to fight, singing and shouting. They waved high their long, sharp, wooden spears, their heavy war clubs, their slings, and their sharp, clamshell axes.

When enemy canoes were seen, coming over the blue Pacific Ocean, the men sprang into their fast canoes. They sailed swiftly over the lagoon to the reef and fought fiercely. They destroyed their enemies or drove them away.

Afterwards, they sat around fires near the house of their chief or under the moon and stars and talked. They acted out their battles, step by step and blow by blow. Around them were the young boys.

The chief's son sat by himself, listening with wide-open eyes. He was not yet fully grown, but he was strong for his age. For hours each day, he practiced fighting—but after all, his weapons were only toys. He struck his enemies—but they were only bushes and trees. It took so long, so long to grow up and be a man and a fighter.

One day, there came from a far-off place a chief named Ranamas. He was sailing among the islands in a long war canoe. He came to find fighters to take back with him to his own island. He stood before the men and their chief in the community house and said, "Oh, men, you are strong fighters! In my land, there is no end to war. Who among you will join my army? Great honor shall be yours."

He told about many fierce battles, but the men said, "We do not care to leave our homes and stay away for a long time."

None of them wished to go. Then the chief's young son spoke up. "Oh, father, let me go!" he cried. "I want to go and fight."

That surprised the men. The boy kept on asking. His father finally agreed to let him go. He was proud that his son was so brave.

"Go, then," he said, "and come back a fighting man."

The boy's mother did not want him to go. "Stay at home, my son," she said. "You are not yet a man. You want a brother or sister, don't you? We might have another child, and you wouldn't be here to see it, if you go away. Wait awhile. Don't go now."

"I'll come home again some time, Mother," said the boy. And so he went with Ranamas to stay away for years.

After he had gone, his mother had another child, a handsome baby boy. "I wish your brother could see you, my little one," she said.

She missed her son greatly. When his little brother was about a year old, she sent the elder son a message.

She picked a taro leaf of small size. With a stick, she made marks on it that were easy to read. The marks told her son that he had a wonderful new baby brother. She asked him to come home and see the child. She wrapped the message in dry bark and tied it with fiber string.

"Who will carry this message?" she asked.

She heard that Ranamas was traveling again among the islands. She went to him and asked about her son.

"Oh, he's well and happy," Ranamas told her. "He has grown nearly to the full size of a man. He is the strongest one in my army. The fighters have chosen him as their Champion, and he leads them in battle."

The mother gave Ranamas the message. He packed it among some things that he carried with him. "Your son shall have the message," he said.

On the way back, Ranamas stayed at night in one place or another. A woman named Anu-aramas invited him to her home. She lived like a human being, but she was really an evil ghost. She had heard of Ranamas and his army. She had heard that the new young Champion loved good deeds and hated evil ones. She knew that he killed ghosts like herself, because she ate human beings.

"Come to my home, great Ranamas," she said in a sweet voice.

She gave him good food and new mats to sleep upon. Then, while he ate and slept, she slyly looked at his things. Soon she found the message that the Champion's mother had sent.

"Aha, aha," she said to herself. "A message to the Champion, my enemy!"

She was afraid to fight the Champion, but she wanted to hurt

104

him. "I'll send him a message that is not true," she said. "A lie is a powerful thing. It can do great harm."

She burned the taro-leaf message. Then she went out and got another leaf of the same size. She drew signs on it, which meant, "You have a new baby brother. He was born a monster with the form of a cat. Come home and see him."

"It will worry the great Champion," she said. "When he hears there is a monster in his family, he will be very much ashamed."

She folded the taro leaf and wrapped it in the covering. Then she put it among the chief's things.

Ranamas went on his way. He gave the Champion the message. The Champion was happy to hear from his mother, but he was shocked when he read the message.

"A monster! A baby brother with the form of a cat!" he said. "I shall not hurry home to see anything like that."

He drew a taro-leaf message to be carried to his mother. He told his mother that he would come home for a visit at some other time.

Then Ranamas went away again. The woman, Anu-aramas invited him to her home again, and he went there. She looked into his things again.

When she found the Champion's message to his mother, she burned it and put another one in its place. She drew signs that told the poor mother a terrible lie. She told her to run away from home secretly and to take her child along. She said that the chief, her husband, was going to kill them both.

The poor mother was frightened when she read it. She told no one. In the middle of the night, she took her child and ran far away from home. She wandered alone in the forest, without food or shelter. Finally, she came, starving and miserable, to a house where people lived. They were kind to her and the child and let them stay there.

The little boy grew fast. One day, after several years had gone by, he said to his mother, "Have I no father?"

She dared not tell him about his father, the chief. So she replied sadly, "You have an elder brother. He is fighting with Ranamas. Oh, I have longed to see him! But he will never find us now."

"I shall go and find him," said the boy.

She tried to keep him, for he was so young, but he wanted to go. "I'll find him and bring him to you, Mother," he said. And so he went away.

He traveled far and long. He asked, many times, where he could find the army of Ranamas. The people showed him the way. They said to each other, "Where did this boy come from? He looks like our Champion. Is he a brother?"

At last, the boy found his brother and the army. The young man and the young boy looked at each other. "Where do you come from?" asked the Champion.

"From our mother," replied the boy. "We are brothers."

"What? You, my brother?" said the Champion. "And you aren't a monster, with the form of a cat?"

"No!" said the boy. "Did you think so?"

"Yes! And I have been sad, all these years," said the Champion.

"Then be glad now," said the younger brother.

The elder brother thought about the taro-leaf message he had received long before. "My mother sent me a lie," he thought. But he said to the boy, "Welcome, brother. I'm very glad to see you. Stay with me and learn to fight."

From that time, they were always together. When the wars were over, the elder brother said, "Come, let's go and see our parents."

Their father, the chief, heard that they were coming. He went to meet them on the way, laughing and crying at the same time.

"Where do you come from, my handsome Champion son?" he said. "I never thought to see you again. Your mother ran away from me. I don't know where she is. And who is the young lad you bring with you? Surely, it's not my younger son?"

He welcomed them both with a feast. They dared not tell their father that their mother was alive and well, for he was angry because she had gone. After several days of feasting, they went far away to the village where she lived. The mother was very glad to see her two sons. "Where did the tall one come from, the one we've never seen before?" asked the people.

"He is my elder son," she said. "And now I have both my boys."

The chief of the place gave the brothers many gifts. He asked them to stay, but they took their mother back to her husband, the chief.

The chief said, "Who told you to bring this runaway woman? She left me and took my child away. Don't bring her here. I forbid it!"

The mother began to cry. Then the elder son said to her, "What kind of a message was that you sent me long ago, telling me that my brother was a monster?"

"Who told you such a lie, my son?" she asked. "I sent you word that you had a fine new baby brother. And why, my son, did you send me a message that my husband would kill me and my child?"

"I sent you no such message!"

The poor woman then said, "Let someone go and get Rana-mas."

When he came, he said that he had not changed the messages in any way. "All I did was to stay in the house of Anu-aramas."

"Then she must come," said the elder brother. He sent his men to get her. The ghost-woman had to come and stand before them all.

The Champion saw that the woman could not meet his eyes. "I believe that you changed those messages," he said.

"Yes, I did it! My lies were stronger than the great Champion," she said at last.

Then the old father, the chief, spoke. "You did a wicked thing. You caused much trouble with your lies. You must die. You are too dangerous to live."

The ghost-woman screamed and ran away. The fighting Champion called to his men, "Catch her and bring her back. She is an evil ghost who has done much harm."

And so they dragged her back, and the Champion killed her.

Then the Champion took his mother and brother to his father, the chief, and said, "Now we can live together and be happy."

The Queen's Snake

There is a long canal in the island of Kusaie. It winds in and out in a strange way. The people tell about it in a story.

Once, long ago in Kusaie, a huge snake lived in a deep cave in the ground at Loal, near Tafwensak village. He had a beautiful young woman with him. Every day, she went down to the beach and bathed and swam by herself. Every evening, the snake came for her and took her back to the cave. The people on the island did not know about her or the snake.

Then, one day, the king of the place said, "I haven't been around the island for a long time. Tomorrow, I'll go with my men and see everything."

They went the next day. On the way, they saw the beautiful young girl near the shore. They were surprised at her beauty, and the king ordered his men to bring her to him. The girl came willingly. The king took her with him to the village of Lellu, where he lived. He made her queen that very day.

As night came on, the snake began to look for the young woman. He looked everywhere on the beach, but she was not there. He went to four different villages. At last, by the sense of smell, he found her in the king's house near the beach in Lellu Village. He laid his head upon a large coral rock, and there he stayed, watching.

Next day, the young lady went to the beach to swim. While running on the shore, she saw the snake, looking at her. She went back to the king's house and brought food for him, but she did not tell anyone. Every day, for a long time, she brought food.

One day, the king looked for her, while she was away. When she came back, he asked, "Where have you been?"

"I have brought food to my old father," she said.

"Your father? Where is he?" asked the king.

"Down near the beach," the queen replied. "Come with me and see him, if you like."

The king went with her. When she showed him the large snake and called him her father, he was frightened. He started back to the house. "Come back with me!" he cried.

"I belong also to my father," said the queen, but she went to the house with her husband. The king thought for a long time about getting his beautiful queen entirely away from her snake father. "She belongs to me. She does not belong to her father at all," he said.

Finally, he said to her, "Your father should live here. Tell him to wait until tomorrow. I will build him a house."

He told every man in the island to come and help to build a long, high house. They worked all night and part of the next day. They built the largest house that had ever been seen in Kusaie Island.

When it was finished, the king said to his young wife, "Ask your father to come into his house."

The queen went to the snake and asked him to the house. He came and began to fill it with his long body. He filled it up more and more. He pushed in, until the house was entirely full, even to the roof. There was not much room for his head. So he broke a hole in the roof and put his head through it.

The next day, the king said to the queen, "Why don't you take a little trip away from here?"

"Where could I go?" she asked.

"The servants go to Tofol to wash clothes in the springs there. Would you like to watch them?"

"Yes," said the queen. "I'll go."

Tofol was a little distance from Lellu, the king's home village. The queen and her servants sailed there in an outrigger canoe. The women washed their clothes and visited with each other. They had a good time.

After the queen had left, the king told his men to bring dry leaves and husks. They brought thousands of them. They piled them around the sides of the snake's house.

"Make a fire all around the house," said the king.

When the house began to burn, a bit of wood ash was blown far away. It fell upon the queen. She looked at it and was frightened. She said to her servants, "We must go back at once. I must save my poor father. Hurry, hurry!"

They got into the canoe and sailed home. When the king saw them coming back so soon, he said to his men, "Take my queen, when she steps out of the canoe. Hold her."

The men stood on shore, with the strongest man in front. When the young queen jumped off the canoe, the strongest man took hold of her. She fought hard and shook away his arm. She ran away so fast that none of the men could catch her. On and on she went, to the snake's house. She jumped into the fire to help her father, and she was burned with him.

The king was sad, for he loved her very much. He was sorry that he had been cruel to her father, but then, it was too late. All his life, he thought about his lovely young queen. He was never happy again.

Some people say that the trail which the snake made, when he crawled along, is now the long canal in Kusaie Island. Whether that is true or not, the canal winds like a snake, and the people are glad to use it.

YOUR DICTIONARY

Some definitions are given here to help you understand new words. The pronunciation of each word is shown by division into syllables, by an accent mark, by marks over the vowels, and sometimes by respelling.

Use the list below. The word after each letter tells you the sound of a vowel. You already know many sounds, including ing, er, ou, etc.

Pronunciation Key

ā lāte	ĭ hĭd	û bûrn
ă ăm	ō ōld	o͞o mo͞on
ä färm	ŏ nŏt	o͝o fo͝ot
ē wē	ô fôr	oi oil
ĕ wĕt	ū ūse	ou out
ī hīde	ŭ ŭs	

A

ache (āk) n. A pain.

a gree' (ă grē') v. To consent.

a light' (ă līt') v. To come down; to settle down or sit.

an' ces tor (ăn' sĕs ter) n. A forefather; a foremother; a relative of greater age than one's self.

an ten' na (ăn tĕn' a) n. A feeler; the horn of an insect.

arch (ärtsh) n. Part of a curve or circle.

a shamed' (ă shāmd') adj. A feeling of being wrong.

at tack' (ă tăk') v. To fall upon with force and weapons.

B

bail' er (bāl' er) n. Something used for dipping up water.

ba' sin (bā' sĭn) n. A hollow dish.

bast (băst) n. Strong, woody fibers.

beak (bēk) n. The bill or nib of a bird.

bit' ter (bĭt' er) adj. Sharp; unpleasant in taste.

blad' der (blăd' er) n. A sac for fluids (in animals).

bless' ing (blĕs' ing) n. That which brings happiness or welfare.

boast (bōst) v. To tell great things; to brag.

111

bo ni′ to (bō nĕ′ tō) n. A fish used for food.

bor′ der (bôr′ der) n. The outer edge; a strip along the outside.

bor′ row (bŏr′ ō) v. To get from another to give back again later.

breeze (brēz) n. A light, gentle wind.

burst (bûrst) 1. n. A sudden breaking out; 2. v. To come out fast and strongly; to break.

bur′ y (bĕr′ ĭ) v. To put into the ground.

C

cab′ bage (kăb′ ĭj) n. A leafy vegetable sometimes chopped up as a salad.

ca nal′ (kă năl′) n. A water course or channel, usually of the same width all the way.

cause (kôz) n. The reason why.

cel e bra′ tion (sĕl ē brā′ shŭn) n. Acts of honor given to a special occasion; a feast.

cer′ tain (sûr′ tĭn) adj. Special among others.

cham′ pi on (chăm′ pĭ ŭn) n. The strongest fighter.

chant (chănt) n. A simple song with a simple tune, usually sung over and over.

cheep (chēp) n. A peep; a shrill sound, as of chickens or birds.

chips (chĭps) n. Small pieces of wood or other material that have been cut off by sharp blows.

chirp (chûrp) n. A short, sharp sound, as of a bird.

chris′ ten (krĭs′ n) v. To give a name to.

clam′ ber (klăm′ ber) v. To climb by catching hold with the hands and feet.

clev′er (klĕv′ er) adj. Very smart; expert.

cliff (clĭf) n. A high, steep wall of rock.

cloud (kloud) v. To make dark.

clum′ sy (klŭm′ zĭ) adj. Without skill; stiff, awkward.

clus′ ter (klŭs′ ter) n. A bunch; a number of things of the same kind growing together.

cock′ le fish (cŏck-) n. A sea animal with a cockle shell (fluted or ribbed shell).

coil (coil) n. A ring, or twist, in hair or rope; or, a number of rings or twists.

com mu ni ty (kŏ mū′ nĭ tĭ) n. A number of people living in the same place.

conch′ shell (kŏnk) n. A large shell to blow into for calling persons, etc.

112

con tain' (kŏn tān') v. To hold; to occupy or have.

cop' ra (kōp' ra) n. Dried coconut meat.

cou' ple (kŭp' l) n. Two of the same kind.

cour' age (kûr' ij) n. Bravery; daring; boldness.

cow' ard (kou' erd) n. A person who is afraid or timid.

croak (krōk) v. To make a low, hoarse noise in the throat.

cru' elty (krōō' ĕl tĭ) n. A cruel deed or act.

crumb (krŭm) n. A very small piece of food.

cup' board (kŭb' erd) n. A closed place.

curse (kûrs) n. A ban; a prevention; a harm.

cus' tom (kus' tum) n. Social habit of thought and action; common usage.

D

de li' cious (dē lĭsh' ŭs) adj. Tasting very good.

de' mon (dē' mŭn) n. A bad spirit; a devil.

de pends' (dē pĕnds') v. Is decided by; hangs upon.

de stroy' (dē stroi') v. To spoil; to ruin.

dis ap pear' (dĭs ă pēr') v. To go from sight, no more to be seen; to vanish.

dis' cov er (dĭs kŭv' er) v. To find; to see for the first time.

dis like' (dĭs līk') v. Not to like or want.

drow' sy (drow' zĭ) adj. Almost sleepy.

E

en joy' (ēn joi') v. Happy in having.

es cape' (ĕs kāp') v. To get away.

e' vil (ē' vĭl) adj. Bad; harmful; wicked.

ex cite' ment (ĕk sīt' mĕnt) n. Action with much feeling.

ex cit' ing (ĕk sīt' ing) adj. Full of action or movement.

ex cuse' (ĕks kūs') v. To leave out; to let go; to pardon.

F

fam' ine (făm' ĭn) n. A time when there is little or no food; a great hunger or starvation.

fa' mous (fā' mŭs) adj. Known to everyone.

fas' ten (făs' n) v. To tie; to make firm.

fa' vor ite (fā' ver ĭt) adj. Much liked; always chosen.

fell (fĕl) v. To cut down.

fi' ber (fī' ber) n. A thread; a tough substance that can be woven.

fierce (fērs) adj. Cruel; wild.

fi' nal ly (fī' năl ĭ) adv. At last; at the end.

flip′ per (flĭp′ er) n. A broad, flat limb for swimming.

flop (flŏp) v. To fall flat or clumsily.

floun′ der n. A flat fish.

flu′ id (flōō′ ĭd) n. That which can flow.

force (fōrs) 1. n. Strength; strong power. 2. v. To drive or get.

for′ est (fŏr′ ĕst) n. Many trees.

for ev′ er (fôr ĕv′ er) adv. Always.

form′ er (for′ mer) adj. Earlier in time or date.

fos′ter brother (fŏs′ ter) n. An adopted brother.

G

gasp (găsp) v. To catch the breath; to pant.

gath′ er (găth′ er) v. To bring together; to bring to one place.

ghost (gōst) n. The spirit of a person who has died.

gi′ ant (jī′ănt) n. A very large or very strong being.

gleam′ ing (glēm′ ĭng) adj. Shining very b r i g h t l y; shooting out light, like a star.

god′ child (gŏd′ child) n. The son or daughter of a person who is like a religious father or mother to the child.

god′ mother (gŏd′ moth er) n. A woman who is a religious mother to a child.

groan (grōn) v. To give a moaning sound, as of pain or grief.

grope (grōp) v. To feel one's way.

H

he′ ro (hēr′ ō) n. A noble leader, especially in story or song.

hoarse (hōrs) adj. Having a rough, harsh voice.

hon′ or (ŏn′ er) 1. n. Good name; glory; good reputation. 2. v. To respect; to think highly of.

house′ hold (-hōld) n. Those who live under the same roof.

howl v. To give a loud cry of distress or a wild yell.

huge (hūj) adj. Very large.

hu′ man (hū′ măn) adj. Having the nature of man.

I

in dus′ tri ous (ĭn dŭs′ trĭ ŭs) adj. Working hard; eager to work and do well.

in tend′ (ĭn tĕnd′) v. To plan; to have something in mind.

in vent′ (ĭn vĕnt′) v. To make up; to find in a new way.

J

jeal' ous (jĕl' ŭs) adj. Wanting what others have; envious.

juice (jōōs) n. A fluid: a liquid; a sap.

L

lad (lăd) n. A boy.

leak (lēk) v. To let water through a hole.

leg' end (lĕj' ĕnd) n. A story coming down from the past.

light' ning (līt' nĭng) n. The flashing of light.

M

mag' ic (măj' ĭk) n. Secret power.

main (mān) adj. The greatest.

ma' na (mă' nä) n. A special natural power, sometimes magical.

man' grove (măng' grōv) n. A tree with aerial roots.

mark (märk) n. Something written.

meal (mēl) n. Some food.

mer' maid (mûr' mād) n. A sea creature with a body that is half woman and half fish.

mes' sage (mĕs' ĭj) n. Word sent out from one person to another.

mes' senger (mĕs' ĕn jer) n. One who carries a message.

mis take' (mĭs tāk') n. A wrong idea; an error.

mon' ster (mŏn' ster) n. A very large person, animal, or thing.

N

naugh' ty (nô' tĭ) adj. Bad; wrong; mischievous; guilty.

neph' ew (nĕf' ū) n. The son of a sister or a brother.

no' tice (nō' tĭs) v. To see; to look at.

O

o be' di ent (ō bē' dĭ ĕnt) adj. Willing to obey or do what is asked.

oc' to pus (ŏk' tō pŭs) n. A sea animal with a large head and a number of arms or tentacles.

odd (ŏd) adj. Different from what is usual or common; unusual; queer.

op' po site (ŏp' ō zĭt) adj. Entirely different.

P

par' a dise (păr' ă dīs) n. A place where souls live after death; a heaven; a pleasure garden.

par' cel (pär' sĕl) n. A package; something wrapped up.

pas' sage (păs' ĭj) n. An entrance; a way; a channel; a place for crossing.

perch (pûrch) v. To sit or rest; to settle down.

pi' rate (pī' rĭt) n. A robber on the high seas.

pit (pĭt) n. A hole in the ground.

plat' form (plăt' fôrm) n. A flat, high place.

poi' son ous (poi' z'n ŭs) adj. Full of poison; full of a deadly thing.

poke (pōk) v. To push.

por' tion (pōr' shŭn) n. A share; a part.

po si' tion (pō sĭ shŭn) n. Rank; a station or standing; a place.

pow' er ful (pou'er fo͝ol) adj. Very strong; great; forceful.

prac' tice (prăk' tĭs) v. To do often.

pre tend' (prē tĕnd') v. To make believe; to sham.

pro tect' (prō tĕct') v. To cover; to defend from danger or attack.

pun' ish (pŭn' ĭsh) v. To give pain because of a fault or a crime.

pun' ish ment (pŭn' ĭsh mĕnt) n. Suffering.

Q

quan' ti ty (kwŏn' tĭ tĭ) n. An amount or portion.

quar' rel (kwŏr' ĕl) 1. v. To speak angrily in a disagreement. 2. n. An angry dispute.

R

raft' er (răf' ter) n. The sloping timber of a roof.

raise (rās) v. To bring up; to cultivate or grow; to lift up.

reed (rēd) n. A tall slender grass; or the stem of a tall grass.

rel' a tive (rĕl' a tĭv) n. A person connected with another by blood.

re spect' (rē spĕkt') n. Favor; honor.

re spect' ed (rē spĕkt' ĕd) adj. Considered honorable; treated as a superior.

re ward' (rē wôrd') n. A prize; pay given for the return of something lost.

rhythm (rĭthm) n. The rise and fall of sounds in written or spoken language.

roam (rōm) v. To go from place to place without any certain plan; to wander.

rough (rŭf) adj. Not polite or gentle; rude.

round' a bout adj. Around in a circle; not straight.

S

sand' pip er (sănd' pīp er) n. A many-colored shore bird that comes and goes; a migratory bird.

sat' is fied (săt' ĭs fīd) adj. Pleased; contented; having what one wants.

scale (skāl) n. A small flat plate, as on a fish.

scat' ter (skăt' er) v. To be separated and go in different directions.

scrap (scrăp) n. A small bit of food left over from a meal.

sea ur'chin n. A sea animal with many very s h a r p spines.

self' ish (sĕl' fĭsh) adj. Caring only for one's self; having great love of self.

shal' low (shăl' ō) adj. Not deep.

shocked (shŏkt) adj. Surprised and frightened.

sir' up (sĭr' ŭp) n. A thick, sweet juice.

smack (smăk) v. To fall down hard, with a smacking noise.

speck' led (spĕk' l' d) adj. Marked with spots.

spine (spīn) n. A stiff, sharp protective thing on a fish, a leaf, etc.

spir' it (spĭr' ĭt) n. Any supernatural being; a being not of this earth.

spout v. To throw out with force.

sprout n. A shoot, a young growth.

squid (skwĭd) n. A sea animal having long arms, or tentacles.

squirt (skwûrt) v. To throw out a liquid in a thin spurt.

starve (stärv) v. To die of hunger.

stir (stûr) v. To move; to set up motion; to rouse, or excite.

strange (strānj) adj. Different; from far away.

strug' gle (strŭg' l) v. To labor hard; to strive violently.

stuff (stŭf) v. To fill very full.

stu' pid (stū' pĭd) adj. Slow, dull in mind; brainless; foolish.

suc ceed' (sŭk sēd') v. To get what one wants; to do something with success; to turn out well.

su' per child (sū' per) n. A child who is wiser, stronger, or more powerful than other children.

sup plies' (sŭp plīz') n. Things needed.

sur prise' (-prīz') n. Something new and not expected.

swash (swŏsh) v. To move, making a splashing sound.

T

tend (tĕnd) v. To take care of.

ten' ta cle (tĕn' tă kl) n. A feeler; a long, flexible feeler on the head of an animal.

tern (tûrn) n. A shore bird, or gull, that plunges into the water for fish.

thigh (thī) n. The leg, between the knee and the trunk of the body.

threat' en (thrĕt' n) v. To promise punishment.

tid' bit (tĭd' bĭt) n. A small piece of food.

tim' id (tĭm' ĭd) adj. Afraid; fearful; not bold.

ti' ny (tī' nĭ) adj. Very small.

torch (tôrch) n. A flaming stick, sometimes carried in the hand.

trail (trāl) n. A track left by something that has passed.

tram' ple (trăm' pl) v. To step hard or heavily.

trick (trĭk) n. An act intended to do mischief or harm or to fool someone.

truth (trōōth) n. That which is true.

tun' nel (tŭn' ĕl) n. A passage through; a burrow.

ty phoon' (tī fōōn') n. A tropical wind storm.

U

un härmed' adj. Not hurt or attacked.

up set' (ŭp sĕt') adj. Disturbed; unsettled.

ur' chin (ûr' chĭn) n. A sea urchin, an animal with many spines, or bristles.

V

vic to' ri ous (vĭc tō' rĭ ŭs) adj. Having won the victory.

W

wan' der (wŏn' der) v. To move about without a plan; to go at pleasure or without control.

weap' on (wĕp' ŭn) n. An instrument for fighting, as a club, dagger, spear, etc.

whale (whāl) n. A sea animal of great size, shaped like a fish.

whir (hwûr) v. To move fast, with a buzzing sound.

whirl (hwûrl) v. To move around and around fast; to turn about.

wick' ed (wĭk' ĕd) adj. Bad; evil; sinful, unholy.

wrap (răp) v. To cover completely.

wrap' ping (răp' ing) n. A cover.

wrig' gle (rĭg' l) v. To twist and turn the body.

wrin' kled (rĭng k'ld) adj. Marked in furrows or ridges; not smooth.

BIBLIOGRAPHY

Helpful background materials were published reports and handbooks of the Office of the Chief of Naval Operations, Navy Department; published reports of the Pacific Science Board, National Research Council, and others; and old-time books and pamphlets, among them the following:

A Chronological History of Voyages and Discoveries in the South Seas, by James Burney, 1764; *A Description of the Islands in the Western Pacific Ocean,* by Andrew Cheyne, 1852; *An Account of the Pelew Islands,* by Henry Wilson, 1788; *A Missionary Voyage to the Southern Pacific,* by James Wilson, 1799; *The Caroline Islands,* by F. W. Christian, 1899; *Voyage of Discovery into the South Seas,* by Otto von Kotzebus, 1821; Books by Luther Halsey Gulick, Missionary, published in the eighteen fifties; *Die Marshall Insulander,* by P. A. Erdland, M.S.C., 1914; *Ergebnisse Der Sudsee-Expedition,* edited by G. Thilenius. L. Fredericksen and Co., Hamburg, 1908-1910.

Background references included: *The Spell of the Pacific,* by Stoven and Day; *The Pacific Ocean,* by Felix Riesenberg; *Native Peoples of the Pacific World,* by Felix M. Keesing; *The Story of the Pacific,* by Hendrik Willem van Loon; *The Exploration of the Pacific,* by J. C. Beaglehole; *Guam and Its People,* by Laura Thompson; *Fortress Islands of the Pacific,* by William Herbert Hobbs; *Study in the Anthropology of Oceania and Asia,* by Coon and Andrews; *The Fortunate Islands,* by Captain Karig, USN; *Japan's Islands of Mystery,* by Willard Price; *America in the New Pacific,* by George E. Taylor; *Island Problems of the Western Pacific,* by Herbert W. Krieger; *Anatomy of Paradise,* by J. C. Furnas; The Infantry Journal, 1945; and others.

Printed in the United States
141254LV00001B/40/A

9 781410 102669